C·E·L·E·S·T·E
·GOES·DANCING·
and Other Stories

An Argentine Collection
Edited by Norman Thomas di Giovanni
Translated by Norman Thomas di Giovanni
and Susan Ashe

NORTH POINT PRESS
San Francisco   1990

First published in Great Britain in 1989
by Constable and Company Limited
This edition published by special arrangement
with the publisher.

Printed in the United States of America

LIBRARY OF CONGRESS
CATALOGING-IN-PUBLICATION DATA
Celeste goes dancing, and other stories : an Argentine
    collection / edited by Norman Thomas di Giovanni :
    translated by Norman Thomas di Giovanni and
    Susan Ashe.
        p.   cm.
    "First published in Great Britain 1989 by Constable
    and Company Limited"—T.p. verso.
    ISBN 0-86547-436-2
    1. Short stories, Argentine—Translations into
    English.   2. Argentine fiction—20th century—
    Translations into English.   3. Short stories, English
    —Translations from Spanish.   I. Di Giovanni,
    Norman Thomas.
PQ7776.C45   1990
863'.0108982—dc20   90-32046

North Point Press
850 Talbot Avenue
Berkeley, California
94706

TO TEDDY PAZ
for twenty years of friendship

Contents

Acknowledgements

Certain of these stories have appeared in the United States in *Fiction Network*, *Translation*, and *Antioch Review*.

'Short Story Contest', written especially for this collection, was first published in *Winter's Tales New Series: 4* (Constable, 1988).

'The Visitation' has been broadcast on the BBC World Service.

Thanks are due to the Fundación Antorchas, Buenos Aires, for their assistance.

Also to Editorial Anagrama, Barcelona, for permission to include the story by Santiago Sylvester.

I am additionally grateful to the following for their help in various ways: Celia Szusterman, Andrew Graham-Yooll, Juan Antonio Masoliver, Jason Wilson, John Jenkins, and Barney Miller. As well as to Edward and María Shaw, in a class of their own as benefactors.

The Argentine painter Antonio Seguí kindly gave permission for a painting of his to be reproduced on the jacket.

Introduction

The short narrative has long been the favoured genre of Argentine writers, who more often than not have used stories rather than the novel to depict the world and their relation to it. A number of Argentine authors have even managed to build considerable careers as writers of fiction on their stories alone. No fewer than six of them in this collection have never written a full-length novel; a seventh, just one. Yet these same seven – Silvina Ocampo, Isidoro Blaisten, Estela dos Santos, Fernando Sorrentino, Angel Bonomini, Santiago Sylvester, and Abelardo Castillo – have together published over thirty volumes of stories.

It is this pre-eminence of the genre that makes the Argentine short story both rich in subject matter and skilled in execution. Jorge Luis Borges summed it up nicely when he said, 'In other parts of Latin America, stories are usually little more than sketches of local colour or social protest – or even an uneasy blend of the two. But in Argentina a story tends to take upon itself all the untrammelled freedom of the imagination.' The high point of this tradition, of course, has been Borges' own celebrated short fiction. And he too never wrote a novel.

In the English-speaking world, particularly in Britain, our curiosity about Argentina should extend beyond the recent violent dispute between the two nations. After all, for a very long time Argentina enjoyed close links with Great Britain. There are some on both sides who even claim that the Argentine was once a virtual colony of Great Britain. The British built and owned the Argentine railways; they settled great tracts of Patagonia; they brought the Hurlingham Club and Harrods to the River Plate. The British community in Argentina had been the most numerous anywhere in the world outside the Empire. The other way round, when in 1852 General Rosas was toppled, he

[9]

fled to Hampshire, spending his final quarter century in South-ampton, where his remains are still buried. To this day the upper-crust Argentine is almost indistinguishable from his English counterpart.

The best way of learning about another country is to read its writers, for they are a nation's soothsayers, its speakers of truth. This collection presents fourteen Argentine writers, many of whom have never been published in this country before and some for the first time in English anywhere. Variety was the chief aim, and towards that end stories will be found here that take place back in the 'twenties (Silvina Ocampo's semi-auto-biographical tale of the artist meeting her younger self) and 'thirties (Estela dos Santos and Alberto Vanasco's bittersweet tango-like evocations, best read, perhaps, with tango music in one's ear); there is also one set abroad (Adolfo Bioy-Casares' Argentine tourist trapped in an almost mathematical puzzle in East Berlin) and another set in a metaphysical dimension (Angel Bonomini's profound meditation on death); there are real-istic stories of tragic irony (Abelardo Castillo's tale of the Indian and the officer lost at the bottom of a crevasse and Fernando Sánchez-Sorondo's about the decline of the old order); there is humour (Marcos Aguinis's greedy, gullible author judging a story contest and Jorge Asís's pedlar of religious pictures); there is poignant understatement and nostalgia for the palmy days (Isidoro Blaisten's account of two minor railway officials from Entre Ríos province); there is bathos with a touch of so-cial comment (Eduardo Gudiño-Kieffer's monologue of the sentimental factory hand); there are stories set in the other Ar-gentina, beyond Buenos Aires, far away in the Andes or in the semi-tropical north (Castillo, Asís, and Santiago Sylvester's impromptu, between-planes party, which may actually take place in Bolivia); there is a touch of Kafka too (Liliana Heer's shy postal employee-pornographer); and there's even an age-old tale with a classic twist (Fernando Sorrentino's dybbuk in suburban Buenos Aires).

Another aim of the collection has been to present stories written or published in the 'eighties. (There is one exception to

[10]

this, Jorge Asís's 'Mule', from the mid 'seventies; my admiration for Asís's sheer story-telling ability made it impossible to leave him out.) I was hoping by this stricture to catch some change, something of the grim hopefulness of a country coming out of the long nightmare of military rule – following a civil war and a defeat in the South Atlantic war – while trying desperately to keep its footing on the path of democracy. But unlike Spain after Franco, there was no radical change from repression to freedom. Argentine writing had been good before the repression and it was good during the repression, whether at home or in exile. Afterwards there was a forced and, thankfully, short-lived polemic between writers who had gone into exile and those who kept writing from within the country. But exile was no guarantee of good writing, and the argument proved false and sterile. In the end good Argentine writing stemmed, as Borges held, from the imagination, wherever that imagination happened to be based.

At the outset, I chose to include only living authors. This left out Julio Cortázar, Humberto Costantini, Antonio Di Benedetto, and Borges. (Worthy story-writers like Haroldo Conti and Rodolfo Walsh were murdered during the repression in 1976.) In the end, the choice represents the editor's taste. Two years ago, with the writer Frank MacShane, I put together an issue of *Translation* magazine devoted to contemporary Argentine writing. That was on a larger scale, with many more writers and with poetry and three essays that were a determined effort to reflect certain social realities. In a way, that earlier selection was a warm-up for this book, which is an entirely personal affair. I simply wanted to present here, in a completely subjective order, a few writers who for one or another reason – a magazine deadline, a dearth of good translators, an Argentine mail strike – had not made their way into that first project and others whom I thought were so good that it seemed imperative to have more of their work in English. Silvina Ocampo was among the former; Bioy-Casares, Asís, Blaisten, and Castillo among the latter.

Several of the contributors have been my friends for twenty

years; others I met for the first time during a long stay in Buenos Aires at the beginning of this year. Only one – Santiago Sylvester, who lives in Madrid – I have not met, though thanks to post and telephone we have become acquainted. It has been a luxury for Susan Ashe and me, as translators, to have been in contact with each author, to have consulted them about choices, difficulties, details. Some of those who know English were even encouraged to comment on drafts of their work. And it has been a pleasure for us too. As Jorge Asís had written to me before that recent journey was undertaken, 'Despite all our problems, Argentina's still a good place for anyone with friends here.' He was right. The Argentine can be counted on to be lavish in friendship.

A dozen or more other writers deserve to be in this book – or in a sequel. I like the work of Bernardo Kordon, Marco Denevi, Daniel Moyano, Juan José Hernández, Ricardo Piglia, Juan José Saer, and a number of newer women writers. Some of them, however, have not written stories recently, and there was another consideration too – the sheer limit of available pages.

In the case of Borges, he is not in this book and yet is on every page. Each of the writers here has read him, and the influence of the Master is telling. Two of them, Silvina Ocampo and Adolfo Bioy-Casares, not only collaborated with Borges in dozens of literary undertakings down through the years but they also shared in working out with him so many basic ideas, stances, and formulations that without the sustained intellectual intimacy among these three we would not have the Borges we know today. As for the others, they learned what I believe may have been the Master's chief lesson – brevity, concision. It never ceases to amaze me how much Argentine writers can say, and with such artistry, in so little space. That concision, of course, Borges himself had learned from the great tradition of British and American writing of the last century.

Borges is here in another way as well. When two decades ago I first arrived in Buenos Aires to work with him on translations into English of his stories, poems, and essays, he was enormously pleased and at the same time slightly embarrassed.

Introduction

Having his own translator by his side and all to himself might appear a touch greedy. So to remedy this, one of the first things Borges set me to do (I certainly was not ready for it at the time) was to put together a collection of short fiction that would make the work of other Argentines known abroad. He gave me books to read and introduced me to a dozen or more of his friends who wrote. He even agreed to collaborate as editor if that would help with prospective publishers and not take the limelight from me. Those writers introduced me to others, and so the circle grew ever wider. But, alas, among the publishers I knew then, I could find no taker. I recently came across that original list. About half the writers in this collection were named there; of the other half here, most had not yet written anything.

Twenty years ago, this would have been the first such collection of Argentine stories to be published in English. Twenty years on, as far as I am aware (and this too does not cease to amaze me), this book is still the first volume of its kind to appear in the English-speaking world.*

Norman Thomas di Giovanni
Gunn, Swimbridge, Devon
19 December 1988

---

* *Postscript, 6 January 1989* – Not so, my erudite friend Jason Wilson points out. An anthology called *Tales from the Argentine*, edited by Waldo Frank, appeared in New York in 1930; it contained, in part, work by Ricardo Güiraldes, Leopoldo Lugones, Horacio Quiroga (an Uruguayan), and President Domingo F. Sarmiento, who died in 1888 and who wrote excellent prose that was not fiction.

THE DRAWING LESSON

Silvina Ocampo

I was fast asleep when I heard a strange noise in the main parlour. This house is very big and so cluttered with objects that some of its rooms are kept closed to prevent them from getting too dirty – or, rather, to prevent them from having to be constantly cleaned – for soot, mud, dogs, and cockroaches, all of which come in from the street, constantly subvert any attempt at cleaning, which, as it happens, seldom or almost never takes place, making it pointless to seal off doors and windows, since soot, mud, dogs, and cockroaches get in anyway.

For a minute or two, I listened hard to the noise, which seemed to be lurking behind the curtains or one of the parlour's ornamental screens. No one could have been up at that hour. The lights were out, and the street door had long since been bolted shut. I got up reluctantly, knowing only too well that by doing so I was inviting insomnia into my night. My favourite thing in the world is sleeping – either when I am happy, because I am happy, or when I am sad, because I am sad. On trains, whenever I travel, or on board ship, or in armchairs, at the drop of a hat, when visitors stay on too long or one of them puts me to sleep, I enjoy nothing so much as impolitely dozing off. (I also enjoy thunderstorms and feeling afraid and when a water-pipe bursts and your bed has to be moved to the other side of the room.) If we hated sleep, I thought, would we go to sleep? No one hates sleep, that's why everyone dies. It's a hangover from childhood to believe that dying is a longing for sleep. I don't want to think about sleep. I was born to draw.

Once up, I pulled my pale-blue dressing gown over my shoulders and, as my slippers had got lost under the bed, I made my way barefoot down the corridors, turning on lights as I went along. I reached the parlour, which was in darkness,

[17]

where I keep the portrait I drew of Gloria Blanco based on Michelangelo's Erythraean Sibyl, a copy of which is pinned to my easel. Trying not to bump into anything that would knock the easel over, I groped for the switch, aided only by the faint illumination – a mixture of moon and electric light from the street lamps in the square – coming in from outside.

Something, a shadow over the pale glow of the night, fell across my path. I did not flinch, as I would have on any other night. Danger, it is said, is itself a protection. Violent crimes, a glimpse of which we get in newspapers, films, magazines, and television, come back to haunt the night in the manner of summer flies – dying, but still full of sound and fury. Fear is a habit of the night. I saw the chandelier, its white opaline tulips like big porcelain teacups. It struck me that for once they did not give me a hankering for coffee or tea or the frothy chocolate we drank as children on national holidays or birthdays. To be thinking about these things in a moment of danger, when someone, perhaps a ghost, had got into the house, did not frighten me. That it didn't should have alarmed me; it was this that was unnatural.

In the half-light of the room my eye was caught by something shining on the floor. I stooped and picked it up. It was a white hair ribbon, the texture of which intrigued me, but what intrigued me more was the fact that my fingers had the sensitivity of touch to tell its colour. Still holding the ribbon, I turned on the chandelier.

It took me a while to see what came as a great shock, for one (meaning me) is slow to react to such shocks. One does not feel the pain of a gunshot wound straightaway. In front of the easel stood a little girl.

She was not pretty, not pretty at all. She wore glasses and had long, straight ash-pale hair. She was so thin that, though not tall, she seemed tall. I saw nothing of her face but her hair and a bit of her forehead. She had on a white pinafore over her dress, and in her right hand she held a piece of charcoal she had taken from the easel. She stared at me without a word. Being shy with

[18]

children, and startled at finding this one in my house at two o'clock in the morning, I felt somewhat ill at ease.

I handed her the ribbon, which had slipped from her hair, but got no thanks.

'Who is it?' she asked with a nod, indicating the drawing.

'Gloria Blanco,' I answered, thinking I must be mad to be replying to her impudent question.

'I don't care who it is.'

'Then why did you ask?'

'I don't know. I don't like your drawing.'

'Who asked you whether you liked it? And how do you know I drew it?'

'I don't. Or, rather, I know only too well.'

'As it happens, I have an army of drawings,' I said. 'They get on my nerves because they take up space, and I don't know why I keep them. I don't like them either. Most of them are portraits, and sometimes they come visiting me in my dreams.'

'That's not the way I taught you to draw,' she said. 'Don't you remember the portrait you did of Miss Edwards – the governess who went mad? She was wearing a velvet choker and taffeta dress. Charcoal was just the thing for drawing her strict face. She used to put my curling pins in at night, wetting the ends of my hair in a glass of water, and then combing them round the leather pads. One time she slapped me when I shouted, "You're hurting me, you're hurting me!" and I pushed her hand away. I still remember that summer day she arrived. I was in the garden with a friend, spying on the new governess from behind a tree. She came in a horse-drawn carriage with a suitcase and a small trunk. We giggled. There was nothing to giggle at. We chortled with laughter. I love to laugh when you're not supposed to. We came out of our hiding place and went to see what was going on. Miss Edwards neither spoke nor understood Spanish, and she kept shouting to the driver, "Please, please."'

'Why did you laugh? It was wrong.'

'Laughter made tears more bearable.'

'So that you used to laugh even though there was nothing to laugh about? I think that's horrible.'

'I do too.'

'But there was nothing funny about her, was there?'

'Not in the least. Her face always looked as if she'd just slapped someone. Which is why it could only be drawn in charcoal, not pencil.'

'You can't draw any face in pencil. Only the church in San Isidro and the boats on the Sarandí, with the sun glinting on the water. With a pencil you can draw water or a church but not the suffering in a face. All faces suffer or have suffered, but only charcoal can draw the shadows of the soul. One day I asked my drawing teacher, "Do you believe in God, señorita?" She hid her face under the brim of her black hat and said, "This part is badly shaded, my child. The light is coming from overhead. You shouldn't talk about God like that!"'

'But I always think about God.'

'A drawing can be made in pencil, charcoal, or India ink. You can use anything to draw.'

'I hate India ink. I sent a drawing called "The Flood" to a monthly magazine; it had to be in India ink. They published it, but what a disappointment! I'd looked forward to it for ages, but when it came out hardly anyone congratulated me, because there was always someone dying or someone getting married.'

'What's your name?'

'Ani Vlis. It's a pseudonym.'

'At your age I'd never heard of a pseudonym.'

'Nor had I.'

'I would like to have seen your drawings.'

'Strange as it may seem, there's one in this room.'

'Show it to me.'

'It's in this portfolio.'

Kneeling, she opened one of the portfolios that I had placed on the floor, since there was no room on the table. She untied the ribbons and took out a big sheet of paper, which she propped on the easel where the other drawing was.

'Look closely,' she said. 'If you'd only drawn the way I taught you, you'd be a great painter. This drawing looks just like an oil painting. Haven't some of our best painters and writers told you

[20]

so? Didn't Figari say, "This child is going to paint very well when she's older, because she sees so poorly"? And didn't Reyles say, "They look like Goya's drawings"? And didn't Pío Collivadino say, "This child is going to be the darling of the whole country"? And wasn't I called "the little queen of all my pupils" by Cata Mórtola? Didn't Quinquela Martín exclaim, "What a wonderful sketch! I wouldn't mind signing it myself!"? And didn't Güiraldes say, "I think she has talent"?'

By nature quiet, she had all at once turned into a chatterbox. She took the stick of charcoal in her dainty fingers and said, 'This is how you use charcoal.'

She was about to sketch a few strokes on the portrait of Miss Edwards, but I stopped her. 'Don't touch that picture. It's fine as it is. It's the only one of my drawings I like. What's more, you'll spoil the Erythraean Sibyl.'

'Your drawing, did you say?'

'Yes,' I said, 'mine. It's the only one of my drawings I like. You don't know what I've been through. It's so long since I've done any drawing. I forced myself to give it up, like giving up smoking. For a time, I woke every morning feeling that by giving up drawing I'd committed a sin. Then I got used to self-denial, to renunciation, to this suicide, this little death. But I wanted to hang on to this picture. Having to stop drawing was like having to stop kissing somebody you love very much and to send him home. That ritual, which had relieved some of the monotony of life, was done with. I'd given up drawing because it made me suffer too much. When I started out, I'd draw a lion and it would look like a dog; I'd draw a horse and it would look like a camel; I'd draw a dove and it would look like a vulture; I'd draw a tiger and it would look like a rat. That was what depressed me more than anything – that my tigers looked like rats. I'd draw a tree and it would look like a feather duster. That was the least of it. I'd draw a shoe and it would look like a toy car. A car? I never tried to draw cars. Just as you do to teach children, I showed grown-ups my pictures pointing out and naming each thing. The hardest part was making people understand that the shading was not hair nor the light a bulge. My

[21]

portraits had no luck. One, of a head exactly like Nefertiti's, which I gave to a member of my family, remained for years stuffed down behind a cupboard. Another, of a very dear friend, disappeared the moment I handed it to him. Yet another grew a patch of mould owing to the damp in the place they hid it. And after all that work, I came to the conclusion that it was better if things did not look so much like what they were. So I tried drawing a lion with a man's face, but I couldn't; and a dog with a sheep's face, but I couldn't.'

'What did it matter? I drew whatever I wanted to draw.'

'It was some time before I realized that reality and art were not the same thing. But it took me too long to find that out; by then I'd got into the mistaken habit of thinking that they were. Sometimes what does one recollect about a thing but its reverse? Is art outside life? The part that is art must serve some purpose. I always suspected that life was a terrible thing; the passing of time terrified me as would the passing of a real lion. I knew I'd be devoured, ring, hair ribbon, pinafore, and all. Miss Edwards sensed it too down by the river one summer afternoon. Sitting on a bench made of branches, she and I talked for the first time as friends. I don't know how the discussion got round to madness. What was it like to be mad? That's the only sentence I remember of that important conversation, which even today seems to me full of twists and secrets. If I try to delve into my memory, what moves me most is Miss Edwards' incorruptible loneliness.'

'Did you love Miss Edwards?'

'I don't know. I thought I loved her. It's happened to me so many times.'

'What?'

'Not really loving someone I thought I loved.'

'Like me.'

'Like you.'

'Are you going?' I asked, for the child was moving away, taking off her shoes to make less noise and placing a forefinger to her lips to impose silence on the two of us.

Catching sight of her bare feet, I held her back.

'Your feet look like mine.'

Her mention of Miss Edwards and everything else she had said revealed her identity, but that our feet were the same brought me up short against real life.

'I was always very fond of you,' I went on. 'To some extent, after I lost my mother, you protected me in her place, but meeting you face to face now I find you treating me like a stranger. Let me tie your hair ribbon. I miss your hair; it was like a fan. You always had a great influence over me. It's your fault that I like paperweights, kaleidoscopes, butterflies, and hammocks.'

'You had a great influence on me too.' She lifted the sheet of paper that lay on top of the copy of the Sibyl. 'One night I dreamed I was lost in the Vatican Museum and saw this face on a vast ceiling. It told me something I didn't understand; I suspect that was your fault.'

She gave me the ribbon I'd tried to tie in her hair.

'Was the influence good or bad?' she asked.

'Good . . . and bad. And mine on you?'

'Bad . . . and good.'

I felt she added the *good* out of kindness.

'All that you learnt I taught you,' she went on.

'You're not exactly modest, I must say. But you're so right! I can love you. I can't love myself.'

'I was never able to love you. I didn't know what you were like.'

She moved away as a human being moves away from a ghost – ever so inconspicuously. She just faded out like the shading in a drawing. I had a feeling that she would appear again – a transfer picture pasted on the night – that she had always been there, like those things one loses but are under one's nose all along, unseen.

'How old are you?'

'I never wanted to grow up. To me, growing older is the worst invention in the world. I felt I would always regret not being the age I am now.'

THE WINDOWLESS ROOM

Adolfo Bioy-Casares

After five or six days in West Berlin, it occurred to me that I was too close to East Berlin to return home without having a look at it. Discreet inquiry, by way of seemingly offhand conversation, convinced me that nobody thought a visit to the eastern sector a rash move.

A few hundred yards from my hotel, I boarded a coach already full of tourists. I remember saying to myself, So long as I stick to this flock, nothing will happen to me. I took the last empty seat. Beside me sat a keen-eyed man with a penetrating look like that of the famous statue of Voltaire in old age that I had seen somewhere or other. My companion was middle-aged, with an olive complexion.

At the checkpoint we changed drivers and guides. Across the border we stopped for a good twenty minutes, right in the eye of the sun, outside the customs and police control point. It was a broiling summer day. One woman complained loudly. When a policeman gave her a prod with his sub-machine-gun and told her to keep quiet the woman looked as though she was on the verge of nervous collapse. Several policemen set out on an ostentatious search of the coach. They looked everywhere, even under the seats, where nothing could have fitted. Scrutinizing passports, they compared faces and photographs. How I envied my fellow passengers, almost all of them American, French, or English tourists, who produced passports with big bright photos! Since mine was out of focus and not much larger than a postage stamp, I went through several anxious moments. The police were not going to believe I was the one in the photograph.

'Keep calm, my friend,' said the man in the seat beside me. 'All they'll do, at worst, is throw their weight about. The police

[27]

here are famous for their bullying, and you know how it is –
when you have a reputation you have to live up to it.'

'Discourtesy to guests always was a mark of incivility,' I said
priggishly. 'A tourist is a guest.'

'When he's not a spy. You don't for a moment imagine all
these Americans, however much they look like farm boys, are as
innocent as they appear?'

'I'm sticking to the facts. The police are taking a long time
over my passport. They barely gave yours a glance.'

'Don't worry. You're an Argentine. That has no reality to
them; it's way beyond the scope of a *tedesco* policeman. I, on
the other hand, am an East Berlin Italian living in West Berlin.
A bit of bad luck, and one of these outings could cost me dear.
Still, here I am.'

The Italian introduced himself. His name was Riccardo
Brescia. He had black hair that he combed straight back, a high
forehead, a steady gaze, a prominent nose and cheekbones,
expressive hands, and a rumpled suit of nondescript brown
cloth. He asked what I did for a living.

'I'm a writer,' I said.

'I'm a cosmographer.'

'That's strange. I remember the first thing that stirred my
intellectual interest had to do with cosmography rather than
literature.'

'And what thing was that?'

'Perhaps intellectual interest is too grand a name for a boy's
natural curiosity. I wondered what the outer limits of the
universe were like. It had to have some shape, some physical
appearance. Because however far away, the universe comes to
an end somewhere.'

'Of course. Did you ever manage to picture it?'

'For some reason, I used to imagine a bare, windowless room
with peeling, mildewed walls and a grey concrete floor.'

'You weren't far wrong.'

'What most bothered me was that beyond the walls there was
nothing – not even the void.'

Without asking permission, some of our tour group began

taking snapshots from the bus – buildings, historic sites, and even people walking by along the street. I was afraid this would stir up a fuss with our guide. No such thing happened, but my nerves, which had calmed down, flared up again.

We stopped in a wide avenue between a row of souvenir stands and the massive gateway to a park. While the guide was explaining that we could have the run of the park for some thirty minutes, Brescia murmured, 'Come with me. I'd like to show you something that will interest you.'

'I don't want any trouble,' I replied. 'If our orders are to walk through the park that's what I'm going to do. As long as I'm with the group, I'll feel safe.'

'Nothing's going to happen to you. This stop will last for exactly forty-five minutes – plenty of time for me to show you something that's going to interest you.'

The Italian was so sure his suggestion was reasonable that I didn't have the strength to oppose him. In some situations the mind obviously works in unexpected ways. What had struck me as madness only moments before now seemed a good excuse for avoiding a long walk. I remember thinking to myself, I haven't come to Berlin to look at trees.

If my memory serves me, we were standing on the top of a very gentle rise in the Berlin plain. While the others set off in a group through the gateway, Brescia and I made our way down a long slope behind the souvenir stalls. At last we entered a street of single-storey houses that reminded me, perhaps because of the small boys kicking a football around, of the outlying suburbs of Buenos Aires. That might once have been me, I said to myself. For some reason, this bit of nostalgia brought back my misgivings. I have to confess that Brescia's voice comforted me.

'My house,' he was saying.

It was a low house with balconied windows either side of the front door and a terrace on the roof. The lock must have been broken, because a chain with a padlock held the double doors together. The Italian took an outsized key from his pocket and opened the padlock. Passing through a dark corridor with a mosaic floor we reached an inner room. I couldn't believe my

eyes. The room was exactly like the one I had imagined as a boy. In a corner was a wrought-iron spiral staircase, brown-painted and blotchy, with an intricately worked balustrade. It led up to the flat roof.

'Well, what do you think, my good man?' asked the Italian. 'The outer edge of the universe, just as you dreamed it.'

'Except that – '

'Of the four corners of this room,' he interrupted me to explain, 'the one with the staircase faces south.'

'A detail that proves nothing.'

'Perhaps. But please look at it.'

'All right,' I said, and I stood facing the corner. 'Now what?'

'I just want you to know that you're living a solemn moment.'

And staring at a cobweb, I almost said. Thick and dusty, it draped the corner a quarter of the way up from the floor. Realizing that Brescia would find this observation facetious, I made an effort to be serious.

'It's quite true that the room resembles the one I pictured, but to say that I'm looking at the outer edge of the world – '

'Not of the world, my good friend.'

'That's what it seemed to me,' I said.

'Of the universe, of the universe,' Brescia went on. 'The whole box of tricks. The entire shooting match – solar systems, heavenly bodies, and stars.'

'Except', I insisted, 'that beyond these walls are rooms and houses.'

'Would you mind coming up to the roof terrace?'

Following him reluctantly, I glanced at my watch. Nearly half an hour had gone by. We mustn't be careless, I thought to myself. The stairs led to a very narrow doorway, a sort of hatch built of dried-out timber and painted grey. We opened the door and stepped out onto the flat roof. It was tiled in red, surrounded by what looked like a white border, which was the tops of the party walls that projected some ten or twelve inches higher than the tiles. There were three more terraces – two opposite and one to the right. All were identical and were surrounded by identical white borders.

'They look like tennis courts,' I said, trying to show that I was still capable of independent judgement.

'Except that each one has a roof door,' he said with a smile.

There was one for each terrace, arranged so that the four huddled round the south-facing corner that, according to Brescia, was the apex of the universe.

'Of course,' I said as if yielding a point, 'this corner is the apex of the four terraces.'

'Are you trying to say that that's all it is?' he asked, and immediately he urged, 'Would you mind going down by one of the other stairways?'

'What are you suggesting? That I trespass? I'm not crazy.'

'It wouldn't be trespass.'

'Do you own all these houses?' I asked with a touch of deference.

'Since you don't understand, trust me and do what I say,' he answered. 'Go down any one of the other stairways. Please.'

'Are you sure I won't be a nuisance?'

'Quite sure.'

Full of trepidation, trying not to make a sound and to see if there were anyone in the gloom, I tiptoed down the stairway opposite the south-facing corner. I found myself in a room exactly like the earlier one, except for a single bewildering detail. It was as if the room had turned round while I was going down the steps; the corner, which I was now seeing from the other side, faced – like the one in the first room – towards the south. There was one still more incredible detail. Down by the floor was an identical cobweb. This cobweb was too much for me. For a minute or two I think I lost my head, and I dashed upstairs, perhaps hoping to expose a fraud. I entered a third doorway, clattered down another set of steps, and again found myself in the same room with the same south-facing corner and the same cobweb down by the floor. Once more I ran up to the roof and went down by the last stairway. I found everything the same, even the cobweb. I was so bewildered that when I heard a voice behind me, I jumped.

'Satisfied?' Brescia asked.

'No,' I said honestly. 'Confused. In each of the four adjoining rooms that same corner faces south.'

'And has the cobweb,' Brescia pointed out.

'However long I stay here, I'm not going to understand. Let's go back to your house.'

I was still afraid that someone might surprise us and think we were thieves or spies. Moreover, despite my confusion, I remembered full well the danger of arriving late at the meeting place by the park gates. I approached the stairway.

'It's not necessary,' said Brescia. 'Come this way.'

I followed like a sleepwalker. We left the room, made our way along the dark corridor with the mosaic floor, and went out into the street through the same door with the broken lock. There were little boys playing football.

'Did all those stairways take me down to your room?' I asked.

'Of course.'

'I just don't understand.'

While making fast the door with the chain and padlock, he calmly remarked, 'It's a good thing you took up writing. The man who gets lost in details will never find the truth.'

'The truth,' I answered, for his remark seemed irrelevant, 'is that if we are not careful we shan't get back to the bus in time.'

I hurried along in a state of anxiety. Not only did my mistake in leaving the group seem unforgivable but I could not understand why I had done it. Naturally, I blamed Brescia; I was pleased to have him at my side, however, in case some policeman questioned me.

We climbed the slope. Down an alleyway we came to the avenue in front of the park gates. The coach was where we had left it, and the driver was talking excitedly to a green-uniformed policeman. I barely had time to step back and hide by the wall of a souvenir stand. Through the gates came the tour group with the guide at their head, holding forth in a loud voice and now and again walking backwards. When the last tourist filed by, I joined the group.

'Come on,' I said to Brescia without turning round.

Back on board the coach, I sank into my seat. My heart was

pounding so that you could hear it. Had the guide questioned me – he looked at me as if he were going to – I would not have known what to say. I had not prepared an explanation and was too much on edge to make one up. The woman who had complained at the beginning of our trip, when we were kept waiting in the sun, complained again and luckily distracted the guide, whose polite reply barely concealed his irritation.

'No, madam,' he said. 'This may not be as beautiful as the places you're used to, but I assure you we shall not keep you here for ever.'

Carefully, so as not to be noticed, I stood up and glanced around. Brescia was nowhere to be seen.

The driver climbed into the coach and started up the engine. If we leave and I say nothing, I asked myself, am I abandoning him? If I speak up, will I give him away? Worse still, would I be laying myself open for one of the tourists to disclose that Brescia and I did not take part in the ramble round the park?

While my scruples alternated with my misgivings, we set off on the way back. Before reaching the border between the eastern and western sectors, I told myself that they were bound to have counted us at the checkpoint; soon they would notice we were one short. Without the slightest problem we crossed over into West Berlin. To tell the truth, I felt relieved. Later on, thinking over my actions, I kept coming to the same conclusion. I had nothing to blame myself for. What could I have done differently? The memory of that afternoon, however, still gives me an uncomfortable feeling just short of guilt.

LOTZ MAKES
NO REPLY

Isidoro Blaisten

Banquo. How goes the night, boy?
Fleance. The moon is down; I have not heard the clock.
Macbeth, II, i

Pecheny woke up. He was propped against the headboard, the back of his neck damp, and he was weeping in the dark. The luminous dial of his alarm clock showed it was very early, and somewhere close by something was about to happen.

Slowly, carefully, he inched to the edge of the bed and with one foot searched around for the trodden-down heel of his slipper. Marité muttered in her sleep. Pecheny turned to her. But Marité's breathing was normal again, slow and regular, echoing the tick of the clock.

In his pyjama pocket, the breast pocket, Pecheny kept his handkerchief; taking it out, he wiped his eyes and put it back. Very close by, something was happening.

Without a sound, Pecheny opened the drawer of the bedside table, felt around, and withdrew a packet of cigarette papers, his tobacco pouch, and lighter. He stuffed everything into his pockets, and at the back of the drawer his fingers touched his Longines pocket watch. He put it into his breast pocket, beside the handkerchief, and stood up. One arm extended in front of him, he groped his way out of the bedroom, brushing against the chest of drawers, brushing against the chair where his white linen summer suit hung. Bands of light filtered through the dining-room shutters. They came from a lantern across the road in a vaulted niche outside Etcheveste's workshop.

Pecheny made his way along the linoleum of the corridor, felt for the folding chair, the magazine rack, the fringe of the pennant, the wall, the kitchen door-frame, and switched on the light. The glare from the oilcloth on the table made him screw up his eyes. The cloth was white, with little blue ducks, and the light rebounded off the white oilcloth, the white wall tiles, the marble draining board, and the spotless white-enamelled paraffin stove. It had happened; it had been very near.

Pecheny pulled up a stool and sat down. He took out the tobacco pouch, the packet of cigarette papers, and his lighter. He placed them in a row on the little ducks. Pulling out his Longines, he opened it, looked at the time, and put it back in his pocket. It had happened at that very moment.

Pecheny looked through the panes of the half-open back door. In the dark he could barely make out the bottom of the garden, the vague shape of the grape arbour. It had happened just then, and Pecheny kept staring at the ducks on the cloth. They were pale blue, with one yellow eye. The water was wavy and yellow. Lotz had a cloth exactly like it. Marité and Teresita Lotz had bought them in a sale at the local department store. Lotz had chuckled. 'Look here, Pecheny, supposing you made a mistake and got into the wrong kitchen. What with these tablecloths, you wouldn't even know it.' Soon, at six forty-nine, Pecheny would have to be with Lotz. He would have to be dressed, ready to leave, setting his Longines, ready to call out, ready to shout for Lotz over the garden fence. Under each duck the wavy line – the same colour as the eyes – was almost imperceptibly broken, and it had just happened.

Pecheny took out his Longines again and left it open on the tablecloth. The lid cast a slanted oval shadow. Pecheny followed the second hand – each leap, each pause, each contraction – listening to each second. There were four and a half hours to go. This was the first time in twenty-seven years' service on the railways that he had been awake at this hour. Maybe that once in Conquistadores. No. It hadn't been as late as this. Lotz would be bound to remember. In four and a half hours Pecheny would be with Lotz, the two of them in their white suits, white panamas, and beige-and-white two-tone shoes.

Pecheny loosened the cord of his tobacco pouch. Now he could see the horse in relief on the leather, its head peering out from the horseshoe with its seven nails, and his initials, E. P. A gift from Lotz. Lotz and Teresita Lotz had given it to him for his birthday. Pecheny slipped a cigarette paper out of its packet and shaped it into a hollowed channel. Spreading the shreds of tobacco out evenly, he rolled it up. Then he moistened the gummed edge. Raising his head, he saw the moon moving behind the shadow of the grapevine. He tore off the gummed strip, smoothed it between his fingers, and put it down on one of the ducks. The duck's eye stared stubbornly ahead. Pecheny lifted the cover of the lighter. Lotz had chuckled. 'Pecheny, no one says flint nowadays. Say lighter. If you say flint everyone'll think you're an old codger.' The flame flared up like an apparition, hung there for a moment, and disappeared into the garden behind the glass pane, behind the night, behind the grapevine. It had happened.

Pecheny took a drag of his cigarette and got up. On top of the radio, on a doily, was an ashtray. He carried it to the table and sat down again. Lotz had one like it but a little paler. It was a present from Redman's. Redman had given each of them one when they went to order Osa's parchment. Lotz had chuckled. 'Well, Pecheny, what do you think of this? We can eat our soup out of them.' 'It's roomy,' Redman had said. The ashtray was enormous, made of reddish-brown bakelite with whitish veins and big white letters all the way round the outside. *Redman's. Concordia. Entre Ríos 719 – 721 – 723. Specialists in Frames – Pictures – Prints – Parchments. Also models for painting and sketching. Direct European imports. Artificial flowers.*

Pecheny turned the ashtray round again, flicked his ash again, looked once more at the stream of smoke drifting out through the kitchen window, and extinguished the cigarette, which by now had begun to come apart. Then he turned the packet of papers round in his hands several times, opened it, and read all the writing on it. *Cigarette papers – 75 leaves. Catfish Brand – Trade mark registered. Tear gently. Selecta & Co, Ltd – Goya. Corrientes. Gummed paper.* Lotz had chuckled. 'When are you going to buy proper cigarettes, Pecheny? Even immigrant navvies don't smoke those things any more.'

Pecheny stared. The Longines gleamed in the light of the high, round, faraway moon. The watch's porcelain face seemed transparent and emphasized the numerals, which stood out in relief. In four hours he would have to be dressed, he would have to be with Lotz, the two of them dressed, leaving their houses, waving good-bye to Marité and to Teresita Lotz from the pavement outside Etcheveste's.

Pecheny stared. Through the panes in the kitchen door, beyond the garden, beyond the privet hedge, above the opposite pavement he saw a pair of bats circling round the lantern. From time to time they hid the light, but he could still read perfectly the words, *Ceramic tiles. La Concordiense. Miguel Etcheveste & Sons. Founded 1916. Terrazzo sinks and paving stones. Reconstituted marble.* Pecheny stood up. One of his slippers caught in the legs of the stool. Lotz had chuckled. 'When are you going to buy yourself real slippers, Pecheny? You remind me of a half-breed.'

Pecheny went to the draining board and lit the Primus. He set the can of methylated spirits to one side and threw away the match. He pumped, he waited, he filled the kettle half-way, he took the canister of maté out of the cupboard. Placing the metal tube in the maté cup, he went back to sit down. Something, perhaps a gust of wind, brought him a waft of poinsettia. Pecheny sat still until the water began to bubble. He went over, turned off the Primus, filled the maté cup and spat the first mouthful into the sink. He left the tap running until the water washed away the traces of maté leaf and the burnt match. He felt as if he was going to cry. He took the kettle, the cup, and a cork mat to the table, and slowly began preparing his maté.

Pecheny drank another maté and leant the tube against the spout of the kettle. He and Lotz would have to be there, one each side of the garden fence, looking at their Longines, setting the minute hand, waiting for the big hand to reach nine, so as to call out 'Loootz,' 'Pechenyyyy.' Sometimes Pecheny shouted first, sometimes Lotz, and sometimes the two shouted together, and then they would chuckle through the fence.

Pecheny took another cigarette paper out of the packet. Through the panes in the kitchen door he could now see the musk roses, the pansy borders, the pinks around the grapevine, and the vine leaves that had begun to glimmer in the half-light. They had been using their Longines for twenty-four years now.

They had been together on the railways two years longer than that – since 1922. The two of them had been promoted in '24. Mr Donovan had sent for them and he personally handed them their Longines. When they had entered his office, Mr Donovan already had the two Longines sitting on his desk. He congratulated the men and made them special inspectors. Their first journey was to Conquistadores, a small town a couple of hours away to the north; later, in Villaguay, they had their picture taken. At a photographer's named Fermoset. They had gone there to have their picture snapped for the Railway Club pass, and the idea had occurred to Lotz to have a comic photo taken in the studio aeroplane. They had it done in boaters, their Longines hanging from their chains, each pointing a finger at Fermoset. They had two copies made. On their return they got them framed at Redman's. Pecheny had put his up over the pennant. The pennant said, *Coarse Fishing Contest. Railway Club Outing. 1947. Concordia – Entre Ríos. Water Sports.* Lotz had chuckled. 'Pecheny, when are you going to buy a reel? You look just like an old-time caudillo with that bamboo pole.'

Pecheny gave a long drag on his cigarette, and the tip glowed. In the niche, the beam from Etcheveste's lantern was hardly visible. By day, you could see there were two lights close together. Soon Marité would wake up. Marité would be alarmed when she saw the kitchen bulb burning, when she saw that Pecheny was not in bed. She would appear in the doorway, fastening her dressing gown, gaping at him, and Pecheny would tell her that it had happened, that he couldn't sleep and that it had already happened.

Pecheny put out his cigarette. He brewed more maté. The maté was cold. He looked at his Longines. Dawn was breaking. So had it been in Conquistadores. It was the latest they had ever turned in in twenty-seven years on the railway. They were playing *truco* in the inspectors' coach. The coach lay in a siding. The stationmaster had come in a sulky to invite them to a barbecue behind his house. His name was Bastián. No, Bastián was the telegraph operator. Lotz would remember. Lotz remembered everything. Lotz had a gift for remembering names.

And numbers. He remembered everyone's birthday. He was the only one in the office who remembered that Osa was retiring. Pecheny and Lotz had gone to Redman's together to order the parchment.

Pecheny turned the ashtray round again. They had travelled up and down the whole branch line in that coach – from Conquistadores to La Calandria, from La Calandria to Federal, from Federal to Alcaraz, from Alcaraz to Diamante. In 1926, they both moved up to Maintenance; in '27, they were promoted together and went into Freight. In Villaguay, they worked either side of the same large desk until the Uriburu revolution, in 1930. The next year they both got married. In '32, they began paying instalments to the Railwayman's Mutual on adjoining houses. In '33, they moved up to head office in Concordia, one desk apart. At head office they were promoted three times, three times in seventeen years, three times to adjacent desks. He would have a shower now. Marité would bring his things to the bathroom. He and Lotz had planted the vines when they moved in. The cuttings had come from Pérsico, down the road. Another neighbour, Parnell, made them the arbours, and Lotz got the waste motor oil that they spent one whole Sunday smearing on the timbers as a preservative. Lotz had chuckled. 'After all this, Pecheny, let's hope the vines grow.' Pecheny would get dressed in the bedroom. He and Lotz would put on their white shirts, their white suits, their polka-dot ties, their two-tone shoes, their alligator belts, their sleeve garters, their watch chains that they attached to their belt loops, their Longines that slipped into their fob pockets.

Pecheny shut his Longines. Now, at five fifty, the two alarm clocks were about to go off. Marité and Teresita Lotz would get up first. They would go into the kitchen to light the Primuses, the heels of their slippers clacking on the lino. Lotz had chuckled. 'They're like two farmyard ducks, Pecheny.' Then they would drink their maté; then he and Lotz would be there, Longines in hand, waiting beside the back fence, waiting for the minute hand to reach the nine, ready to call out. As Pecheny called out, raising his head, he could see Lotz's poinsettia

[42]

tangled over the fence with his. Then each would walk down his garden path, skirt the bed of pinks, the pansy border, open their little gates, and together greet each other. 'How're things, Lotz?' 'How are things, Pecheny?' And they'd cross the street. Under Etcheveste's niche they'd turn round and wait for Marité and Teresita Lotz, who would come to the garden gates, each wearing gauze headscarves over hair rollers, each wearing a polka-dot dressing gown and marabou-trimmed mules. First they would greet each other. 'How're things, Teresita?' 'How're things, Marité?' Then Marité would call out, 'How're things, Lotz? Bye, bye.' Teresita Lotz would call out, 'How're things, Pecheny? Bye, bye.' And, walking a few steps backwards before turning round, the two men would give a wave. Then they would walk up to Parnell's joinery, cross at Pérsico's, take the short cut by the wall around the bottling plant, and at seven fifty on the dot they would be at head office, signing in.

Pecheny stood up. It was daytime now. He slid the stool under the table, turned off the light, and put away his Longines. Then he heard Teresita Lotz cry out. It was a long, despairing cry, a call to them. She was shouting from the bedroom, and her cry came over the back fence. Not hurrying, Pecheny went to find Marité. Through the window, as he made his way down the lino of the passage, he saw the poinsettia, a vivid red in the first light.

JAVIER WICONDA'S SISTERS

Fernando Sánchez-Sorondo

To my father

On the seventh of February 1950, Javier Wiconda, who lived out in the country ten miles or so from a ramshackle backwoods village, received the following telegram: 'Your sister dead. Await your arrival. Mama.'

The first thing Wiconda did was to make his way to the little settlement – from which a neighbouring farmer had brought him the wire – to find out which of his three sisters the message referred to. It was no good. No one at the post office could do more than express their sympathy. Nor was there any news of the Wiconda family from their solicitor Ezequiel, who was just back from Buenos Aires.

The first thing Javier thought, or felt, cannot be recorded here without the risk of error. So, ignoring the order in which his thoughts, feelings, and emotions surfaced, let us just say that, back in the country again and still not knowing on which sister to focus his grief, Wiconda pitted his mind against the facts.

Seven years earlier, shortly before his thirtieth birthday, Wiconda had moved from the capital, where his family lived, to a house that a century before had been one of the outbuildings on their country estate. Here his father, whom Javier had come to appreciate – as the old man himself had predicted – only after his death, and his shadowy forebears used to spend the summer. Their portraits still adorned the walls, arranged, like mementoes of death, in the order of their decease. Here the jacaranda and mahogany furniture (Javier's bed, for example, which had given shelter to generation upon generation of dreams) perfumed the silent rooms with an age-old fragrance, rivalled only by that exuding from the yellowed pages of old story-books that had fed the childhood imagination of those ancestors.

[47]

Javier Wiconda's Sisters

Here he was then, elbows propped on his ebony desk, face to face with the grim brevity of the telegram that lay before him. This telegram, he mused, like others before it, might very well have got lost in the post, in which case he would never have known a thing. That such blessed ignorance might have been was his first piece of subterfuge. Perfecting this line of reasoning, he relished the conclusion that his sister had not died.

His sister had not died; but unexpectedly, lurking like a dog behind a gate, the truth suddenly barked at him, and that afternoon his sister – which one? – died again.

The careless handwriting on the telegram later gave rise to another subterfuge: it was, Wiconda projected, just another of the well-known pranks devised by the old boy at the post office, who bordered on imbecility. In the relentless monotony of the pampa, it seemed almost understandable that the postmaster might from time to time stir people's minds with just such a bucket of cold water. Hadn't the old man been a shade too sorry for him?

But Wiconda's trip into fantasy became gradually untenable; from the precarious perch of his deliverance, he looked down with a new-found calm at the firm ground of the facts. By six o'clock in the evening, depressed by the absurdity of his fantasy, he accepted the absurdity of the truth.

One of his sisters had died, and he didn't know which. The west wind blew open the window of his room. A weak ray of sunlight fell on to the far wall, whose double doors deflected it hither and thither. With the interrogative accuracy of a blackboard pointer, the sunbeam picked out, one after another, the photographs of his sisters that hung on the wall. Cynthia – a fair-haired child stroking her white angora cat with enormous concentration. Luisa – bright eyes narrowed in disdainful impatience at the camera. Teresa – a face distended in a grin.

He got up, closed the window, saddled his horse, and two hours later was in the village. He bought a bus ticket and took a seat beside the window. It was eight o'clock; in eleven hours' time he would be in Buenos Aires.

The bus set off, trailing an ever-growing cloud of exhaust

[48]

behind it. Alongside the road the poplars were becoming one with the night. The artificial daylight of street lamps spread over the plain. It was that hour when the countryside increases in size, concealing behind its everyday appearance a fleeting, magic essence that gives only a hint of itself and that holds us in a state of bewildered ecstasy, as if we were in the presence of someone trying to deliver a supernatural message in a supernatural language.

No sleeping draught could have worked on Wiconda. His memory turned first to Cynthia, the eldest. In his bus seat, sitting uncomfortably, he uttered her name, and his sister appeared to him in her brown fur coat, her blonde hair knotted by the wind. They were at the dockside; Cynthia was going abroad. Cranes looked out towards the river, fearless iron giraffes. A ship's beautiful name. People embracing as if for the last time. A photograph's magnesium flash on a ready smile. Cynthia babbled in a way he had never seen before, out of control, writhing like a snake that has just been dealt a mortal blow, laughing excitedly; she was talking with her hands and eyes as if she were a conjurer pulling words out of her sleeve. She had not been able to stand the silence into which Wiconda withdrew in the awkward intensity of his feelings. On the deck of the ship, lamps were being lit; slowly, Cynthia grew smaller and smaller in the evening and larger and larger in Wiconda's heart, as the huge white mass drew away to the accompaniment of war-hardened nautical commands.

He had another memory of Cynthia, and then another, and another. It was a summer night in a garden. White swing seats, magnolias, a furtive ruffle of wing-beats amongst the treetops. At Cynthia's table a timid specimen of a man appeared to be insulting her; Wiconda had rushed to her defence. He remembered Cynthia's smile (her lips took no part in it), with which she said as he came up, 'Forgive him.'

Deeply, unopposed, mental pictures of Luisa and Teresa worked their way into his memory. Luisa's voice and the youthful boisterousness aboard the bus vied for Wiconda's attention. Luisa was, her voice measured, her look measured. Once more, as in the past, he rummaged in his sister's desk: exam papers written by Luisa's pupils – under the stern seal of the national emblem – and corrected by her with an energetic red pencil (The Rout of Cancha Rayada, very good, 10; An Autumn Morning, fair); a crucifix; a surrealist poem; and everything else randomly offered by those chaotic drawers. He remembered her taking her place at the dining-table, her hands covered in chalk dust, her gentle voice battered by the class-room. He saw her return from her labours – she was studying philosophy and teaching Spanish – demand a meal on the spot, toss off an analysis of love (charitable love, sexual love), and depart. He saw her on oppressive summer days, smartening herself up in front of a mirror for the school prize-giving; he saw her mannish shoes, he saw her slapdash make-up; and he felt sorry for her and wept as he saw her march off briskly with her speeches under her arm and that slow bead of sweat that crept down her face and then blended into skin.

Would he ever see Luisa again? Would he ever meet her walking along, enduring her femininity as if it were a judgement?

And Teresa, little Teresa, his youngest sister, whose birth he had watched and whom he had taught the colours and the alphabet. Whom once a month he had taken on outings to the zoo. Who would look after Teresa's six children now? Whose skirts would they hide behind when they visited their grand-mother in the big house? Who would cheer up the big house with shreds of childish laughter or the news, at almost regular intervals, of a new member of the family?

Wiconda tried to concentrate on the details of the journey. He looked out but found only his own face reflected in the window. With wilful curiosity he checked the time. His fellow passengers, who at the outset had sat primly upright from long training, were by now used to the bus and no longer tried to hide their weariness. They lounged about, and a privileged few had put their legs up on the seats, giving the bus that exhausted look of a bar early in the morning, when the chairs are on the tables.

Stretching his limbs, someone yawned out the name of a stop. Having put many hamlets behind it, the bus at last reached a city.

Wiconda shot out of his seat in search of a telephone. Hopeless. He'd have to wait fifty minutes for a line, he was told. The bus would be on its way again before that. The night was humid and gleamed like the skin of a seal. He went to the bus-stop café and ordered some tea. The other passengers, who by this time had struck up friendships, laughed and chatted in voices born of a long journey. The bread had the same sour taste as his gullet, down which it forced its painful way. Tiny specks of Flit, stuck there by the damp, made a pale curtain on the café window.

Boarding the bus again in the deep darkness, the dregs of the night, he once more found Cynthia there beside him. It was like that time when, to scare her, he had struck a chord on the lowest octave of the estate's chapel organ. Cynthia was there beside him, and they had turned to look at each other in mutual terror.

It was at this point, in a tortuous attempt to bribe fate, that Wiconda made the vow. If Cynthia was not dead, he would carry her off to the country and surround her with peace. They would rebuild their secret hideout in the greenhouse, where Cynthia used to come on her skewbald mare after lunch when she was supposed to be resting, smuggling in a stock of palm-honey liqueur, ham, and dry biscuits that tasted of sacking. They would inhale those alfalfa dawns again, getting up – as in the old days – so early that they could hardly pick out their horses in the dusty dark of the corral before they galloped off through the mist, Cynthia singing her head off. Her misfortune, the blow she had suffered, they would leave buried, like the crop that is finished and ploughed under, until the fresh soil of Cynthia's childhood could take over again. If she was not dead, he would rescue her from that hateful city and carry her off to the country.

A sudden sense of guilt overwhelmed him. He felt that his lamentation over Cynthia had a fratricidal implication. He felt that he had made a choice, that he was acting the executioner.

[51]

He tried to remember and did, but to no avail, the way his mother had taught him as a child to send himself to sleep – close his eyes, press the lids together, and concentrate his blind stare on his nose. He got up from his seat and walked down the aisle. While he stalked about, hideously awake, like a watchman in a threatened building, the other passengers slept so soundly that the bus seemed empty.

Returning to his seat with a feeling of drowsiness that came to nothing, he resigned himself to having all three sisters appear to him together in a discordant clash, like different melodies radiating out at the same time. Cynthia, Teresa, Luisa, Cynthia, Cynthia.

After that, the abominable night. The minutes filing slowly past. And everything that was yet to come: the doors he would have to pass through, the number of times he would have to say good morning before he found out the truth. And the certainty that, whether he liked it or not, he would go on living.

At six o'clock in the morning the bus reached the plodding Buenos Aires outskirts, sad as a Sunday, with smells of frying, damp doorways, and frowzy young girls leaving for work unmoved by the mindless stream of wolf-whistling. Wiconda felt detached from these things, cut off like a sleepwalker. A tawny house, a playing-field, a man – each appeared through his window as silent and random as a throw of the dice on a gaming table. The journey had drained him of all anxiety, and he felt worn out now, as empty as if he had never existed. Since he did not know which of his three sisters was doomed to die, he had slaughtered them with Herodian injustice and had mourned them all.

The rest he remembers dimly, as if someone else had told it to him. The rest belongs to the following day, whichever day it was that followed the unforgettable day.

Through a mass of identical faces and garments, through ritual embraces, he made his way into the drawing-room, where he found his mother. In a listless voice, she asked why he hadn't come at the first news, when they wired him how seriously ill she was. He did not understand. He did not know what his

[52]

mother was talking about. (Perhaps she was talking about one of those telegrams that might well have got lost in the post and that perhaps had contained the name that could not be uttered.) 'It was a heart attack,' his mother explained. While he let her embrace him, Wiconda wondered if some time – not now, of course, but some time – he would solve the riddle.

Around the coffin, shuffling knots of visitors mingled and drew apart, apparently unable to decide on a suitable place or stance. The coffin lay at the rear of the house in the little music room where the harp had stood. Two hostile weeping women (whom he dared not look at) and the drone of litanies hemmed him in. With disconcerting calm he took in his sister's corpse. At last he knew which one it was, even though it was Cynthia.

CELESTE GOES DANCING

Estela dos Santos

Celeste washes the clothes, cooks the meals, irons the clothes, scrubs the patio, waters the pots of geraniums and pelargoniums, goes to the tangerine tree to test the ripeness of each fruit, which she picks at exactly the right moment, listens to soap operas, two every afternoon and one in the evening, sings along with the radio whenever the radio's playing a song, boleros and mambos, sambas and tangos, jingles and commercials. She forgets the lyrics, changes them, hums them, stops whatever she's doing, cocks an ear, and learns them all over again.

In the late afternoon don Albino goes out to shop, brings back two big bags, and sets them down in the kitchen doorway. Celeste unpacks, potatoes in the bin, tomatoes in the ice-box, steaks on the marble draining board, a sprinkle of salt, and that's them ready for the grill. In the evening Pedro comes home, takes a bath, leaves his clothes strewn on the floor, shaves, douses himself in cologne, combs his hair, smarming down the waves, dons his Prince of Wales suit, and out he goes.

Picking up his clothes, Celeste inspects collar and cuffs. If a shirt has another few hours' wear she smooths it out and hangs it on the back of the chair alongside Pedro's bed. The rest goes into the washtub at the far end of the patio where the bathroom is.

In the cool of the night, in the silence of the neighbourhood, Celeste sets a small chair outside the front door, gazes into the darkness, greets passers-by. The leaves hang limp. When they stir she catches the movement, not taking her eyes off them even for a second. Don Albino draws his chair up close to the kerb, raises his voice just a shade to tell his neighbour over the way what he thinks of the weather and the cost of living. At midnight the sound of scraping chairs and stools retreats down passageways, the last lights go out, don Albino quaffs lemon juice to thin the blood, while in her low chair Celeste dozes on.

She wakes from a dream and goes to her room for her second sleep. Another dream wakes her, and Pedro's mumbling in his cot. At seven in the morning, closing the wardrobe door with its long mirror, don Albino disturbs her third sleep. Sun, street noises, laughter from the back yard, shouts of children out in front rouse her from her fourth sleep. Celeste shuts her eyes against the light, greets the day, goes into the kitchen, and clutches the table to hold herself up, recovering the balance she lost in the night, the thread that will lead her firmly into her housework.

Her dreams intrude on her normal routine. Celeste races along a lighted road, body aching, legs aching, they buckle, she can't run another step, she struggles on because from somewhere out there she's being called, *I'm coming, I'm coming*, she can't manage another step, *I'm coming, I'm coming*, she falters, not another step, the light conceals her.

Celeste trips along, a flower in her hand, reaches the graveside and leans down to place the flower in the little vase in front of the photograph of herself dead. She's about to put the flower down but in the picture, instead of a lively face, the wisp of a smile, and the plait of hair wound round her head like a wreath, all so familiar to her, she finds clouded eyes, a half-open mouth, an inclined head, and her First Communion veil. Celeste tries to straighten up. She can't put a flower on her own grave, she can't, she tries to straighten up.

First get out the milk, pour herself a cupful. Cold without sugar tastes better. Then iron, there's the pile of clothes. Wash the clothes in the midday heat, it cools you. The plants are watered when the sun goes down.

Listening to her radio serials in the afternoon, Celeste lies naked on the brass bed. When she gets tearful, she wipes her nose on the bottom sheet. She falls asleep looking at the characters in the Last Supper, picking them out one by one. Then, to the right, Saint Joseph with his ear of wheat, and to the left the Sacred Heart. The heart's there, you can touch it with your hand as there's no glass. The glass shattered the night doña Asunción died. Celeste had come running, the Sacred Heart was bleeding, the blood spurted over the bed, over don Albino's shirt, seeping out in the washtub and turning the water to blood.

Celeste stretches her arms out and flies, the wind ruffles her clothes. Celeste lowers her arms, covering herself, and hurtles down, down, she's going to crash to the ground, she's going to crash.

Celeste does not dust the furniture. Every Saturday she watches closely as don Albino cleans the little bottles on the dressing-table, the hand mirror, the powder box, each one of doña Asunción's jars. Bursting into sobs when she was told to dust them, Celeste hid her tears and said all the things would be broken, and she dared not touch them. She doesn't make the beds either. On Saturdays don Albino changes the sheets and hands them to her. The brass bed in the middle of the room and at the foot of it, one each side, Pedro's cot under the window and Celeste's cot.

The open door of the wardrobe lights up the dark. Celeste looks at it from her bed. There she is in the mirror, making faces, talking into it. She stands on the bed and begins to dance. She's perfect. Celeste dances like a ballerina. She knows how to. At seven o'clock don Albino gets up and shuts the wardrobe door. After that Celeste falls into a peaceful sleep, a deep, deep sleep.

'Take me to the dance, Pedro. I want to dance.'

Don Albino clutches his daughter around the waist, tries to make her take a few steps, but Celeste goes stiff and pulls away from his arms.

'How can you want to go dancing if you don't learn to dance first?'

Behind the left-hand door of the wardrobe hang two of doña Asunción's dresses, long ones. Celeste opens the door, takes a quick look at them, then closes it again. Below the dresses, on the floor of the wardrobe, lie two pairs of doña Asunción's shoes, high heels. In the upper part of the wardrobe, on a shelf, are two boxes with two hats of doña Asunción's, with ribbons. Celeste never opens the boxes. She quickly shuts the door again. Celeste holds the wardrobe door shut with all her might, she lies on the floor and holds it shut with her feet. Big and flat from always going about barefoot, her feet cover the whole door. *You're not going to open, you're not going to open.*

The door opens. Celeste opens the door from the inside, hat boxes on her head, dresses and shoes on, and, dancing, she treads on Celeste's body, stamping and stamping on her, the heels drilling her, drilling her.

In the cool night air, Celeste puts her little chair out on the pavement. She greets the passers-by. Everyone's passing by. *Good evening* (that one's going to the dance), *hello there* (you're going to the dance), *so long, Pedro* (you're going to the dance), *go to bed now, everybody's gone out, go to bed, daughter, and lock up behind you* (he's going to the dance). During Carnival everyone goes dancing. The radio will be at the dance.

In the wardrobe mirror Celeste dances too. She dances perfectly to the sound of the radio, dances everything you can dance, never putting a foot wrong. Celeste gets up, she turns on the light. She opens the left-hand door of the wardrobe, takes out the shoes, and tries them on. One pair, another pair. She'll wear these. She takes down the dresses. One dress, another. She'll wear this. She takes down the boxes. One hat, another. She puts this one on. She shoves the clothes off the chair and sits in front of the dressing-table. She lifts the lid off the powder box, dabs powder on her face, takes out the lipstick, paints her mouth with it, opens the jar of rouge, puts rouge on her cheeks, opens the jar of blue eye-shadow, puts eye-shadow around her eyes. She takes the stopper off the perfume bottle, puts perfume on her throat, behind her ears, under her dress sleeves, sprinkles perfume on her clothes. She stands in front of the wardrobe mirror. Celeste raises her arms and dances. She dances to the sound of the radio. She dances everything the radio plays and never puts a foot wrong. Celeste dances perfectly. All she needs is a partner. Celeste grabs at the mirror, she tries to take Celeste by the waist. She bursts into tears in

Celeste's arms. She picks up the hem of her dress and dries her wet face.

Celeste sets out for the dance. She walks along dark streets. Arms try to encircle her. *Where are you off to, little girl? Come with me, little girl.* Celeste flies along the dark streets, and nobody can touch her. Celeste reaches the dance. Arms try to hold her back. *Where are you going, little girl? Ticket, little girl*, but Celeste goes flying in, light-footed into the middle of the dancing couples, everyone's dancing, light-footed among the dancing couples, everyone's dancing in couples, Celeste glides alone across the dance floor, and the music stops, and everyone stops.

Celeste stops. Couples draw apart. Celeste squeezes her way into the front row of women, all of them looking straight ahead at all the men, who squeeze together looking straight ahead. The men step forward, they take hold of the women, a man takes hold of Celeste. All the couples dance, the music guides all the couples, including Celeste and the man holding her, who treads on her feet, who heats her face with his breath. The couples collide, feet are trodden on, the man takes Celeste by the waist, and, an arm still around her, draws her outside, where you can feel the air.

'Little girl, it's so hot in there I don't know how they stand it. What about some beer?'

Celeste drinks beer. It's not iced. Warm beer's like piss.

'On your own, are you? Whatever you ask for, it's hopeless, everything's warm. What's your name? The ice-boxes can't keep up. You from around here? It's the first dance you've been to, that's what I think. In Carnival, you should enjoy yourself. You like tangos or mambos? You slipped out tonight, that's what I think. Don't you have one of those little mirrors? Take my handkerchief, your make-up's running. In Carnival, who cares. You were right to slip out. You've got to take risks. What's your name? You've got a secret. You're a strange one, you are. Where did you get that hat? No one wears them nowadays. At this time of night, they'll be looking for you. I'll bet they keep you locked up. Cat got your tongue? Deaf and dumb, are you? Little girl, you've come to me from heaven. The minute I saw you, I said this one's for me. Heaven-sent. In all the din of Carnival, you can't be alone. Deaf and dumb, are you? Really deaf and dumb? Take off those shoes, with those heels you can't even walk. Where did you get them, dummy? Throw them away. I wonder how people stand it in there when it's so much cooler out here. There's nothing like the cool night air when it's so hot. I love sleeping outdoors on the grass. You don't know how nice and cool grass is. Are you deaf? Really deaf? You were made for me. All my life I've been looking for you. That's why I came here. I had a feeling. Once I had a feeling and my grandfather died. I knew it. It scared me. But I'm not scared now. How old are you? Lie on the grass. Feel it, feel how nice and cool it is. Take my handkerchief, wipe your mouth. You don't need make-up, little girl. Where did you get that stuff? From your mother's dressing-table? Will they be looking for you? Where are you from? You fell into my lap from heaven. I had a feeling, and I was in there about three hours, sweating away, when I saw you. You came because of me. I'm not afraid any more. I like you because you keep quiet. You're not like the others, you dumb little, quiet little thing. That's why I like you. I'm not going to hurt you. You soft, sweet little thing, you little sweetheart.'

Celeste howled, she howled like a dog, Celeste's howls filled the park. She growled like a tiger, the trees shook, she yowled like a wolf. The wind buffeted the two bodies, made their hair stand on end, made cars in the streets stop with a squeal of brakes, tore down the power lines, devoured the man.

Celeste tried to wake up because she felt cold. She was in a park. Celeste came and covered her eyes with her shoes. The soles pressed against her eyelids. She couldn't open them but she heard the birds, the sun, the trees, the ants. The grass was stirring around Celeste, it rustled, tiny insects ran up and down her legs, climbing her body, looking into her face. The ground moved under Celeste, got into her mouth, Celeste spat it out and tried to get up, but Celeste put her big feet on her chest and couldn't.

Celeste walked along the sunlit streets, her feet aching, pinched, burnt by the hot pavements, her dress dirty, her hat shapeless. She brushed the leaves and insects off her dress but never finished the job. She wanted to get home to wash it. She walked and walked, she asked the way, and no one answered her. People stared and laughed. Celeste sat down on a doorstep and began to cry. When she'd had enough of this, she wiped her face on the hem of her dress and went on walking and asking the way. No one answered her. She walked and walked along sunlit streets. Turning a corner, she had a bucket of water thrown over her. She stumbled, whimpered, then she wrung out the skirt of her dress to dry it. She walked and walked, she asked the way, a couple took her by the hand, they told her they didn't know but they'd take her to the police. Behind them came a swarm of boys singing strident Carnival songs.

The couple turned, they let go of Celeste, they ran at the boys. Celeste waited there without moving, refusing to walk unless they held her hand. They left her at the police-station desk. A woman came to see if she was, Celeste grabbed her hand, *it's not her*, said the woman, she let go and went away. A man came to see if she was, Celeste grabbed his hand, *it's not her*, said the man, he let go and went away. A married couple came to see if she was, Celeste grabbed their hands, *it's not her*, they said, they let go and went away. Don Albino came, he took her by the arms and shook her, he slapped her hard. A policeman came along and took him by the shoulder, *don't hit her, don*, he said. They went out into the street, one in front of the other, don Albino ahead, Celeste behind. They went home.

NEITHER SAINTS
NOR SINNERS

Alberto Vanasco

Neither the passage of time nor the incursion of motorways has managed to do away with the old boarding-house on Montes de Oca where Basilio and Jacinto lived. 'Lived' is a euphemism. In point of fact, because they owed two months' back rent, they spent most of their time stealing in and out of the place, and whenever they weren't going anywhere they locked themselves in their room and tried to make no noise. They even went to the bathroom on tiptoe, although they could be seen as they passed the big archway that led into the dining-room.

It was in the course of one of these furtive journeys to the bathroom that Basilio overheard a telephone conversation that don Reinaldo was having in a corner of the living-room. Although deaf as a post, don Reinaldo still managed to talk on the phone all day to clients or friends, which led the brothers to conclude that electrical impulses from the receiver went straight to the old man's brain. This deafness of his, however, was what gave the boys a certain freedom of movement within the house, since doña Epifanía, don Reinaldo's wife, had little taste for staying in and doing housework.

It all started on the afternoon Basilio eavesdropped towards the end of one of don Reinaldo's telephone sessions. The old man was shouting so loudly that even sitting in the bath the boy could hear every word. Don Reinaldo was betting on the horses, which he did every week, and he repeated the name of his favourite once or twice, as if it was the other person and not he who was deaf. He had picked a filly by the name of November who was running that Sunday in the sixth race at Palermo.

Back in their room, Basilio told Jacinto what he had heard, and immediately the two of them began to evolve fantasies about what they might get up to had they the money to put on November and were November to win. But, as usual, spurred on by hunger and other pressures related to their lack of funds, they soon forgot all about the matter until chance once again offered them the opportunity to strike it rich at the racecourse that Sunday.

It happened on the Saturday, on their way back from the centre of Buenos Aires, in a tram jam-packed with human flesh, in which passengers perched on the running-boards and clung from the driver's platform. This, however, was not the fact that was to change the lives of the two perennial students. They were so used to travelling out to Barracas squashed like sardines that such conditions meant nothing to them. What was unusual was the fact that all at once two seats close to them were left vacant when an old couple stood up and made their way forward to get off.

Wide-awake and quick off the mark, Basilio and Jacinto plunked themselves down. It was a comfort they did not often get to enjoy. But something on the seat dug into Jacinto at the base of his spine – something hard, bulky, and smooth. Feeling behind him in annoyance, he took hold of the object but as soon as he caught a glimpse of it he shoved it back out of sight.

What he had seen was a big, old, fat wallet tied up with a rubber band. Not saying a word, he shifted so as to be able to slip the wallet under his jacket and from there slide it around to where he could grip it under his arm. Jacinto gave no sign to his brother until they got off at the corner near the boarding-house. There he pulled Basilio behind a tree and showed him what he had found. The pair could not believe their luck and laughed and laughed, hugging each other and dancing round the plane tree. The shabby wallet was stuffed with enormous brand-new one- and five-peso notes.

They stayed under the tree for nearly half an hour, not knowing what to do and afraid that at any moment the wallet, money and all, would vanish into thin air. Finally coming to their senses, they marched straight home and into the living-room, cheerfully greeting don Reinaldo and doña Epifanía and one or two of the other lodgers. Back in their room, they carefully counted the money, arranging the notes on the bed in little piles according to denomination. There was enough to place any number of bets. You could almost hear their minds working out how much they would win at odds of twenty or thirty to one, then at forty, fifty, and so on. Their eyes, which had narrowed in the mental effort, still sparkled between their half-closed lids.

'It's bound to pay over forty to one,' said Basilio.

'That's for sure,' agreed Jacinto.

'But ...' Basilio went on. They both fell silent, probably thinking the same thing.

'But what?' asked Jacinto after a while.

'Nothing.'

'Don't tell me nothing, say what you're thinking.'

'Did you see that old couple whose seats we got? They were ancient and they couldn't have looked poorer.'

There was a pause.

'Not that old or poor, really. What about all the money they had on them?' Jacinto said.

'Yes, that's true enough. I got a good look at them; they were fairly ordinary.'

'You think so?'

'Definitely.' There was another pause. 'But the wallet was old and shabby.'

'You're right,' concluded Jacinto.

'There's one thing we could do,' Basilio suggested finally. 'In the wallet was a slip of paper with a name and address on it. Let's find out what kind of house it is, rich or poor. That way we can rest easy. If it's a nice house we can keep the money.'

'That sounds like a good idea,' said the other.

The two boys accepted this brilliant solution with some relief. They had no intention of profiting at the expense of a poor old couple. On the paper, written in pencil in big faint letters, was an address at the far end of Caaguazú Street, way out in Lanús Este.

'We'll go there tomorrow and give the money back,' Basilio said when he realized it was a neighbourhood where poor working people lived. 'They must be worse off than we are.'

'Then where did this money come from?'

'Maybe it was a loan from someone.'

'Hang about,' Jacinto insisted. 'There's no rush. What if they live in a mansion and are millionaires?'

'All right. Tomorrow we'll find out.'

Early the next day they caught a tram straight to Lanús Este. Half an hour later the vehicle was creeping along unpaved streets lined with little houses flimsily built out of bits of wood and galvanized iron and open on all sides to the wind and rain. Out in front were tiny yards of baked earth and straggly plants. From the tram window, Basilio and Jacinto saw ever more undeniable signs of extreme poverty and grim destitution filing past.

'Bye bye, little pile of money,' said Basilio as they arrived. 'Get out the wallet; we'll have to give it back.'

'Not so hasty. Maybe they own the whole neighbourhood,' replied Jacinto.

The tramline ended in a square, and they had to get out and make their way along a miry street for another three blocks, until they stood in front of the house they were looking for. It was not a house as much as a shanty made of mud bricks, a sort of rundown shack that had stubbornly held its ground while the suburbs mushroomed all around it. Its iron gate had sprung its hinges. The two layabouts exchanged rueful looks.

'Wait,' said Jacinto. 'Don't tell them we found the wallet, and let's see whether they really need it. Rich people are eccentric. God knows why, but maybe these two like living here.'

Just as they knocked the same crone they had seen with the old man on the tram appeared in the doorway. She snivelled and dried her tears on the corner of her apron. Unable to think of anything better, the two rascals said they were reporters.

'Ah, gentlemen from the newspaper,' sobbed the woman. 'So you know already? Poor Ignacio, losing his money like that. I think he left his wallet on the tram. What a calamity! It's going to be the ruin of us. Come in, come in, and see him for yourselves.'

In they went and saw the man lying on his bed with a tattered sheet pulled up to his nose. He seemed either asleep or stone-cold dead. The two reporters quietly took up position at the foot of the bed, while the old woman began sobbing again. Basilio tugged at Jacinto's sleeve to tell him to hand over the money, but Jacinto wouldn't and shook off his brother's arm, pulling away from him. They scuffled for a few seconds until the wallet fell to the floor and together they crouched down to pick it up. Half out of sight behind the foot of the bed, they tried to find a solution.

'You'll have to give it to her,' whispered Jacinto.

'Let me have one more minute,' Basilio hissed.

The two old people heard them but did not understand what was going on. The woman stopped whimpering, and from his deathbed the old man opened one eye. At last the two rascals made up their minds.

'Look, señora, we aren't really reporters,' explained Basilio. 'We're the ones who found your wallet and we have come to give your money back.'

The elder brother's words had a remarkable effect. He had barely finished his sentence when the old man leapt up out of the bed as if shot from a cannon and snatched his wallet from Jacinto. At the same time, the wife bent down and opened the bottom drawer of a small, rickety wardrobe, the one stick of furniture in the room. The drawer was crammed with bank-notes of all colours and denominations, and with a single bound don Ignacio was on the spot, adding the pesos from the wallet to those in the drawer. Basilio and Jacinto thought that they had lost their minds, that what they were seeing was an hallucination or a dream. But in no time this feeling turned to anger.

'Do you realize,' the old woman said, 'that we had been to collect our rents and we'd lost every penny of our money? My husband would have died if he hadn't got that drawer filled this month. Do you realize that?'

The two layabouts realized.

'That's the absolute truth,' explained the arrogant old man – almost dead, but now of joy – dancing about in the long nightshirt he had worn in bed. 'It was just what I needed; thanks to you the drawer is full.'

The woman showed them into the kitchen, where she began brewing maté. As it happened, the brothers did not drink maté, but now, to gain time to cook up a plan of action, they decided to make an exception. No sooner had he sucked up the first bitter mouthful than Basilio had a splendid idea.

'Don Ignacio,' he said, 'wouldn't you like to double your money and fill another drawer?'

The old man's pupils contracted to tiny points, whether out of suspicion or greed it was hard to tell. On the spot, the two visitors told him all about November, about the excellent odds, and about the horse's being a sure thing. The sixth race began at six o'clock that afternoon and it was now three. Don Ignacio was quite happy to have filled only one drawer and had no intention of risking his savings. His wife agreed and brewed more maté. Basilio and Jacinto summoned up all their powers of persuasion, the same ones they used on doña Epifanía month in and month out, and for the next hour they chipped away at don Ignacio's misgivings. In the end, when they told him that by putting half the money on each way they could not lose, because even if the horse didn't win they would still stand to collect, the greedy old man's resistance gave way – moreover, he began to wax eager and in addition to the money from this month's rents he took out of the coffer at least as much again. Finally, they managed to get him dressed, and clutching two big bundles of banknotes they made their way out into the street. Basilio and Jacinto favoured going to the station to catch a taxi, but to don Ignacio the premature squandering of such a large sum seemed an extravagance. There was no other course than to take the tram and surrender themselves to the vagaries of the Transport Authority.

Once more they crossed the city at an agonizing crawl, trying to keep don Ignacio amused, since at each stop he wanted to get off. The Riachuelo drawbridge was raised, and they had to wait a quarter of an hour while a coaster chuntered by before they could go on. But not for long. Crossing San Juan, the tram conductor stopped to argue with a taxi driver who had come to a halt on the line, and only when, led by Basilio and Jacinto, the passengers began to protest did they continue. By then it was almost five o'clock.

At a little before six, they were outside the racecourse and they rushed in, practically carrying don Ignacio between them. In their haste, they went to the wrong window and instead of putting their money on November, who was number eleven, they put it on number ten. Realizing their mistake at once, the boys said nothing to the old man, hoping the horse they had bet on would win. But it didn't. November came in neck and neck with number five, and it was a photo finish. When number eleven was declared the winner, the old man collapsed on the spot, overcome with joy, leaving the brothers in the thick of the crowd with a dead man on their hands and not a penny to their names.

SHORT STORY CONTEST

Marcos Aguinis

Eduardo flung his coat at the sofa, let out a weary sigh, and said he was going to tell me an amazing story. His face wore a grim look, yet at the same time he radiated a distinct glow. When I offered to get him some coffee, he put an imperious halt to it.

'Later,' he said. 'Right now sit down and listen.'

He unbuttoned his collar and sat back. Before he could get going, his hand waved away the words that were fighting to come out of his mouth. His eyes, which had grown small and bleary, told of the effort he was making to set his complicated tale in order. In the end, he opted for asking me whether I'd ever judged a short story contest.

I shrugged. Sure, several times. Why? Because, he said, momentarily carried away, what had happened to him had never happened before in any competition since the year dot. His mistake had been – maybe it was his vanity, maybe the money – to accept too readily and then to find himself smack in the midst of an uncontainable muddle. He wasn't exaggerating, he said, just airing his chagrin. And his partial joy.

I couldn't follow him, but neither could I hide my curiosity.

Eduardo is an obsessive writer who has achieved a moderate success with his two novels and four story collections. He's manic about his style and, to his publisher's despair, pitiless about last-minute tinkering. Scouring his first book for its few typos – three, to be exact – so affected his eyesight that he was forced to visit three oculists in the space of a single month and then to swear an oath never to reread anything he had written once it appeared in print.

Years back, he told me, he'd had to judge the offerings of a local group, but, as a contest, that had been a nonentity. When he'd been approached this time, what bowled him over was the huge sum of money he was offered as a fee. Although tempted, he feigned lack of interest, since the sponsor of the affair was a new supermarket whose public-relations man thought he could exploit literature to draw customers.

I interrupted Eduardo to say one couldn't help seeing posters about the contest. Buenos Aires was plastered with them.

What he most disliked, Eduardo growled, was this coupling of supermarkets and creative writing, of literary genres and mass-produced foods, the debasement of fiction to make people buy sausages. He disliked it and, what was worse, he was stupid to dislike it, because these days literature itself was mass-produced, and short stories and novels were on sale in any supermarket.

No, it was he who was behind the times, he who was inconsistent. This became only too plain to Eduardo on the day he met the PR man to sign their agreement. While trying to put on the air of a connoisseur of the arts, the man came out with one or two clangers that turned Eduardo's ears red. But the man also handed over a fat advance that delighted Eduardo, though at the same time it filled him with shame. Knowing he was in it only for the money, how could he then condemn the supermarket man for promoting this literary extravaganza only for the money?

In the next few weeks, before any of the stories were submitted, Eduardo had tried to put this surrender of his principles out of mind. Besides, who was going to write a story on a topic as inane as the one stipulated by the PR man – The Supermarket in Today's World? This genius's sole concern was retailing, and it didn't matter to him one dried fig or one tiny tin of peas that anyone might possibly want to write about something else. He was sure there'd be a flood of entries. However, in the event that there wasn't, the important thing was that the competition should make an impact. The company would guarantee a winner, and under no circumstances would the contest be declared null and void. After all, the PR man was not going to forgo the trappings of the presentation ceremony, when he himself would confer the diploma, the medal, and the resounding cheque.

The vehemence with which Eduardo recounted the affair amused me. It was a short story in itself and maybe the best one that would come out of the contest – a story of stories, or metastory, as those who specialize in eviscerating literature might say.

While he waited for the manuscripts to arrive on his doorstep, Eduardo found growing in him an abhorrence of assembly-line techniques, which insidiously force to the wall all craftsmen, among whom he numbered the writer; an abhorence of PR men, whose diabolical mission it is to corrupt natural relationships for the purpose of making money; an abhorrence of contests, which hold out the promise of reward for merit and end by breaking the promise and making a nonsense of merit; an abhorrence of bad writing, which he was soon to be gorging on; an abhorrence of himself for condoning the theme of the contest; an abhorrence, in short, of the whole damned thing. I could imagine Eduardo sticking his fingers down his throat to make himself spew up all his most deepseated aversions.

Two months passed, and Eduardo had spent the best part of the advance. Then, one day, there arrived a cardboard box emblazoned with the shining emblem of the contest and containing twenty-eight stories, together with a short and sweet letter from the PR man. Eduardo was astounded. He had not expected so many entries; surely, it had to be a load of junk. What else could anyone write about supermarkets?

Flipping through the folders, he read some of the titles. 'Honey and Waffles', 'A Colourful Saunter', 'The Joy of Shopping Carts', 'The Diet of a Superstore Buff'. Eduardo's first reaction was to shut the box and hold it shut tight for several minutes to prevent its noxious contents from getting out and polluting the air. Then he tore the letter up into small pieces and threw them one by one into the wastepaper basket.

The first unfortunate upshot was that for several days he couldn't write a word. Or read. Instead, he racked his brain for ways to break the contract, though by now he could not pay back the advance. In this straitjacket and unable to think clearly, Eduardo refused to swallow the folderfuls of tripe. Such lethal outpourings of unmitigated hogwash, he feared, might damage his brain cells.

[79]

His wife Irene tried to reason with him, but to no avail. After a week or so, he once more dared open the box, which he'd hidden in the farthest and darkest corner of his study, hoping the mildew would make inroads on it. This time he spotted other improbable titles, such as 'Jesus Goes Shopping', 'The Extraterrestrial Supermarket', 'Adventures of a Tinned Man', and 'Supermarket Baby'.

Shutting his eyes, Eduardo picked out a story at random – 'The Victory of Samothrace'. A title with classical associations, a reference to antiquity, a certain respect for the arts. Perhaps this one was palatable.

'What an old fool you are, Eduardo!' Eduardo shouted at himself. What had the Winged Victory to do with a supermarket? Or, put another way, how clever the writer must have been to link the two. Eduardo was assailed by conflicting ideas. Had he been too reactionary before this and was he now falling over himself to compensate for it by feeling sudden sympathy for the contest? Tales inspired by shabby street markets were legitimate enough. Why not give expression to the experiences and daydreams inspired in people today by ample shopping-carts, fancy packaging, well-trained checkout girls, and the mingled aromas of both homely and exotic products?

Eduardo scanned a few more titles: 'The Supermarket Inferno', 'A Grocer's Guide to the Galaxy', 'Love Among the Chocolates', 'The Kinky Checkout Girl', 'The White Wine Murders'. This was more like it, he thought. A touch ingenuous, perhaps, but not bad. Who could tell, it might even prove to be the style of our times. The new was always irritating and disagreeable at first – but only at first. Since signing the contract, some of Eduardo's cherished beliefs were showing cracks. He could accept that contemporary writing might be evolving in the direction of a supermarket genre, but was he cut out to write it?

His spirits sank when, to his surprise, he received a second box, containing a further thirty-six stories. Even Irene was dismayed, and she had to make a fresh effort to find words to soothe him. Hadn't the first twenty-eight stories been the total number of entries? Hadn't the submission date closed? Apparently not. Another sixty-five boxes arrived at Eduardo's house, each with about thirty folders, making a grand total of some two thousand short stories.

It's an outrage! A scandal! A swindle! groaned Eduardo. It's a colossal success! rejoiced the PR man in his latest note, short and sweet as ever.

Titles began swarming in Eduardo's head: 'The Terrorist Lollipop', 'Sex and the Delivery Boy', 'The Egg Smugglers', 'Yoghurts of Death'. He gargled insults and spat them out like grapeshot at the supermarket's PR man, who was the most despicable, cynical, parasitic creature under the sun and who had not only snared Eduardo with money but was out to make him work like a slave, to the last drop of sweat, for the fees that had once seemed so generous. Just the thought of the mountain of dross his brain would have to absorb pressed on Eduardo like a weight.

While Eduardo read, Irene did her best to keep the boxes and folders in order. Like unwanted guests, they seemed to be constantly shifting about from place to place, monopolizing chairs and beds and driving their timid hosts into corners. Irene was relentless in keeping a few passageways free, but she was unable to dislodge the piles of folders from bedroom, bathroom, living-room, or kitchen.

At the beginning and end of each tale he read, Eduardo grumbled that he would never be able to read two thousand stories. Still, he forged ahead. 'The Jewel in the Beetroot' he found ingenious and quite well written; 'Store-room Romance' gave him a chuckle; and 'Saccharine in the Carry-cot' he thought poignant. But the rest were mostly dreary, cliché-ridden, and fit only for stoking the boiler.

Within a day or two, Irene stopped nagging him about doing the job properly, and Eduardo took to reading far into the night. His earlier derision now turned to addiction. Exhausting page after page, his eyes grew bloodshot from words and metaphors, baked beans and derring-do, caloried seductions and futuristic settings, pedestrian language and the occasional high-flown phrase. He looked for genuine creativity but settled for mediocrity and ineptitude so long as a work was even remotely original in its portrayal of human conflict. One story in twenty-five or thirty was.

A handful of tales verged on science fiction, and in one the supermarket's drug section offered for sale ampoules of dehydrated semen with which women could perform do-it-yourself insemination in the comfort of their homes. The back of the package listed the baby's genetic traits, and the product came with a choice of applicator: the plain economy model or the electronically controlled, easy-to-operate inflatable doll with a selection of nineteen different styles of love-making.

Another story along similar lines dealt with a game from the toy section. Its object was to select sets of chromosomes from a glossy leaflet and combine them to construct beasts from the mythologies of ancient Egypt, Greece, and India. A more expensive and ambitious version of this game, designed for several competitors, involved a computer to concoct new monsters. Soon terrifying beasts emitting hideous sounds were proliferating in children's rooms, running amok and threatening a bloodbath. In the end, the scale of a Leviathan short-circuits the computer, painlessly vaporizing a child's arm.

Irene had advised him to read the first few lines of each story, to proceed obliquely through the subsequent pages, and not linger unless the piece were any good. Surely this was the way all contests were judged the world over. By then, Eduardo had found it impossible even to read this small amount. But after 'The Absentminded Stocktaker', 'The Erotic Depilatory', and 'Takeaway Mythology', something changed. Now he became as meticulous in his reading as he had hitherto been in his writing.

Just as he got through half the folders, the PR man telephoned to remind Eduardo that he was to come to the office in three days' time to confirm the winning entry. As a prestigious writer and as a member of the prestigious panel of judges, Eduardo was, after all, a living symbol of Argentine literature.

Eduardo felt an attack of palpitations coming on. There was no way he could finish the hundreds of remaining stories. He babbled a plea for an extension.

Impossible, replied the PR man, because the ceremony at which the fabulous prize was to be presented had already been announced. He went on to cite the television channels that would be providing coverage and the guest stars who would be in attendance, and he assured Eduardo that to a gifted writer like himself three days were more than adequate in which to spot the talent from among the thousand stories Eduardo still had not got around to reading.

In three days, then, a van would come from the supermarket to collect all the stories, which, as a further gesture of the company's meticulousness, efficiency, and courtesy, would promptly be returned to their authors. Eduardo felt more panic-stricken than ever.

Irene massaged the back of his neck. In three days he'd also get the rest of his money, which was the reason he had got involved in the first place. But Eduardo didn't mind having the money later if only he could finish reading the stories. His wife found this incomprehensible. The contest had upset their daily routine, their love life, their married bliss, and now here was Irene having to call a doctor, for suddenly Eduardo was struck down by a violent bout of diarrhoea.

Sedatives were powerless to relieve his galloping anxiety, and during the doctor's examination Eduardo could not tear his eyes from the nearest folder. Throwing up his hands in despair, the doctor told the patient he must choose between his health and an absurd sense of fair play. Eduardo said he no longer cared about fairness or about who won. What interested him was rescuing those few good stories dotted like nuggets of gold among the bad ones. The doctor, however much he scratched his head, was at a loss to fathom Eduardo's passion.

It was a passion that went unrewarded. The van arrived on time. Two men and three women burst into the apartment and set about searching every nook and cranny as if engaged in a police raid. So Eduardo felt it; so Irene wanted it. Every last folder was collected, even those hidden in drawers, under the sofa, and between books. Doubled up with diarrhoea, Eduardo forced open one or two boxes and tried to slip a few folders under the carpet. But the round-up was both thorough and relentless, and every last morsel was spirited away. Now story-less, Eduardo swallowed more pills, but to no avail.

He shaved, put a roll of toilet paper in his briefcase, and set off for the supermarket. The PR man welcomed him with a big public-relations smile. He sat Eduardo at his desk and sur-rounded him with three secretaries, or bodyguards, or hired actors. Which, Eduardo couldn't tell. The three kept shoving papers under his nose – the endless list of entries, a copy of the contract Eduardo had signed months before, the diploma for first prize with the winner's name already on it and underneath the signatures of the PR man and a local dignitary. All that was missing was Eduardo's signature.

The contest had been a tremendous success. It was already the talk of the neighbourhood, and after the ceremony would be the talk of all Buenos Aires. Eduardo baulked. He hadn't been able to read all the material. To which the PR man replied that it was superfluous to go over all that again, since the conver-sation in which Eduardo had asked for an extension had been duly taped. The request was in serious breach of the clause in the contract committing Eduardo to finish his reading within two months. Of course, the supermarket was more than willing to overlook this point, nor would it ask for its money back.

Brandishing a cheque-book, the PR man waited for Eduardo to put his signature to the diploma. Then the cheque could be written and the tape destroyed. After that, the man said, he would shake Eduardo's hand and invite him to enjoy the grand ceremony, where before his very eyes he would behold the massive boost in his prestige as a writer. There was no question of Eduardo's playing the ivory-tower purist and refusing to award the prize to the supermarket's choice just because he hadn't read half the manuscripts. After all, the PR man's tender smile seemed to say as he held out the cheque, you went into this job like a whore and came out of it falling in love.

'Now, then,' Eduardo finished, 'how about that coffee of yours? I think I could use it.'

YOU'VE GOT A NIPPER, DON'T YOU?

Eduardo Gudiño-Kieffer

You've got a nipper, don't you? All right, that's just a way of putting it, I know. It ain't really you as has it, it's the wife has it, know what I mean? It's her indoors gets the worst of it, poor thing. First there's your nine months coming over all queer and bringing everything up, then her swelling out and you trying to convince her you love her just the same and women big up front are lovely and she's got prettier in a different way, a prettier way of getting prettier, a cosier way, more like a flower, more like a fruit, more like a garden and all – only more, loads more. Anyhow, you ain't going to tell me the one what gets the worst of it ain't her, especially the last part, when it comes to the real graft. And that's your actual graft, the hardest of the lot, and don't give me none of your modern painless childbirth ballocks. That's a load of old cobblers doctors come up with to line their pockets. Childbirth is the worst pain you can have, and it's got to be like that 'cause God said so and he even wrote it down in the Bible.

But that don't have nothing to do with it. What I'm trying to say is a baby's made inside the woman. 'Course, without the father it wouldn't be there, would it? Though the only thing the man does is pump something in and have a bit of fun. After that, the foetus and all, that's up to the mother and nobody else. Even so, the father feels he's the father and if he don't actually have the little beggar inside him sometimes it's just like he does. It's not your physical feeling, it's your moral thing. And as it's a moral thing you could say as the baby's his. 'Course it is. Look at it like this, the kiddie's born and he ain't much more than a shrimp of a thing what kips all the time. And as all he does is kip morning, noon, and night and he don't weigh seven pounds and can't be more than twenty inches long, you suddenly think stone me, is he breathing or is he breathing and if he ain't breathing he's snuffed it and what'll I do? So you tiptoe round and put your hand over his nose what ain't no bigger than a bean and you feel the warm little breath. Only then do you relax, realizing at the same time that even though it was the missus what had him inside her so long he's your kiddie too, the father's. It's there in your mind even though you don't say it 'cause it ain't what your average bloke talks about, is it?

The thing is all the time she was in there having little Oscar I felt really rotten, only I never let on. We was all down the hospital (which to my mind they ought to call the inhospitable what with that smell of ether and all), the whole lot of us, the wife's mum and dad, all her brothers, and me own old lady what's a widow. Hah. Says she, but I reckon she never had no husband, only I don't say nothing. Why give her aggro at her age? The mums (mine and the wife's) were the only ones, so they says, what ever come through it with flying colours. But I tell you, I wanted to puke something awful, only you don't want to know about that, just thinking about my poor Yoli in all that pain and agony. Fact is, I really thought it was me feeling the pain, never mind all that being a man stuff, and if I ever told my brothers-in-law what I was feeling they'd have cracked up. But just you wait till it's their turn. They're single now and don't know bugger all but they'll find out soon enough, believe you me. The only one what understood any of it was me father-in-law, old don Nicola, bless his cotton socks, who takes me off to the little bar round the corner, orders a couple of coffees, and says, 'Looka, better you taking it nice and easy, son, nice and easy and it'sa going to be fine.' It always got up my nose how he still speaks that Eyetie lingo when he's been here since the Ark, but this time he could have been one of them poncey actors you see on the telly what can make you cry your blooming eyes out.

And it did come out fine, even though our Oscar was a bit on the skinny side. Not quite seven pounds, like I said, which ain't much alongside Baroni's nipper, him coming to work puffed up like a pigeon 'cause his was a ten-pounder. But the doctor says to me, Cabrera, he says, it's a lot better, fat babies have less defences. First I thought here's another load of cobblers like what they all gives you, but, straight up, since my Oscar was born I reckon the doctor was on the level. I always thought fat ones was healthier and I remember my auntie Matilda, God rest her soul, saying, 'Fatter they are, the more beautiful they are.' But it seems like all that's changed now, fatness is out, and you got to be thin from the day you're born. It's better, your scientists have proved it, ain't they? Now I'm quite thin meself, and that's why a lot of these fatties don't half envy me. I'm tickled pink young Oscar's on the skinny side 'cause it means he's going to take after me. Besides, if you think about it, why'd the doctor want to have me on? If he says being thin's better, then it must be true. He ain't going to make money out of that so why should he give me a load of hogwash?

Fact is, I was dead chuffed. Am I going to complain when baby Oscar turns out to be a chip off the old block, with a real little cock on him and all? When the doctor says to me, Cabrera, he says, it's a boy, and the nurse holds him up to the window, I was so dead chuffed poor Yoli went clean out of me mind. It wasn't till I saw her that it dawned on me what she'd had to go through to push out the little beggar what's her very own but mine too. And so I says to her, Yoli, I says, bearing in mind I don't know if she can hear me or not what with the anaesthetic and all, I says Yoli, you ain't only my missus now, you're the mother of my son, and just for that I'm going to give you more respect than what you ever had before. Straight up, that's what I said.

There I was, so over the moon it was coming out of my ears, and stone me if it ain't just then I have to go down the works and walk into a right cock-up. Never mind being over the moon and wanting to invite me mates out to wet the baby's head, I had to get stuck in. 'Cause the lads was right, the wage negotiations had been a complete wash-out. With pay rises like they was offering, we weren't going nowhere, and now, on top of that, here I was with a nipper. And to feed a nipper you need the readies. After an eight-hour slog and not a grumble out of us, it's our right. Anyway, that's what they're always telling us in their speeches. It's one of your fundamental basic rights, innit?

[89]

But not in the eyes of some. Management said it ain't, and even the old bill said it wasn't. Search me why the bill said that when every other day you read in the papers how some copper topped himself 'cause he can't make ends meet, not to mention how they're shitting themselves, getting done over or machine-gunned from some passing car, and all the time the public don't give a monkey's and some even like it 'cause the old bill ain't exactly your flavour of the month, are they? It must be the uniform or maybe it's that when you was a nipper your mum was always telling you just you watch out, my son, or I'll have the copper on you.

But that's not what I wanted to say. I wanted to tell you a bloke's got the right to do better for himself, though there's some as thinks different. I ain't no bleeding genius but I know there comes a time when you've had it up to here and you got to wade in and take some action. That's why when Zanotti said we had to take over the works ourselves we all agreed, meself included. There weren't no other way. Sure, I'd have liked to have stayed in that night to watch Yoli feeding young Oscar, but what could a bloke do? If you think about it, the lads taking over the works is protecting our interests, and protecting our interests is protecting my interests, and protecting my interests is protecting young Oscar's – it's protecting our Oscar. So instead of going home I stay on, and Zanotti tells me to keep an eye on them lads in the Militants and not let them make no trouble or nothing but just stay put, taking no orders that don't come straight from him. His actual words was that don't emanate directly from him. Only I said 'come' 'cause that's plainer like, innit? I wish I could talk fancy so's I could tell you how it was being there at night in the works with them Militant lads. I was with five of them, and it was another world, know what I mean? It's something you can't imagine if you ain't never seen it, a great sort of silence, machine-made like everything else down the works. Your kiddies now, they ain't machine-made.

I was there all night, I was. Vergara had brought tea and a Primus and we sat up drinking the stuff until a milky daylight began to creep over everything. That's when the Tannoy started up, and first thing they're playing the National Anthem. The National Anthem, I ask you! Passing round the tea, we didn't know whether to stand up or stay sitting, 'cause respect's respect and we all know you stand up for the National Anthem. But this time we couldn't, we didn't dare. If they'd a seen us from out there we'd have been dead ducks. Then the Anthem ends and a voice says, 'You in there, come out with your hands up.' There's a long, long silence and then they says again to come out with our hands up and that's when we hear Zanotti's voice shouting that he's coming out first, on his own, to talk. I peek out the doorway of the wing where we are, and I see Zanotti, just like he said, come out of the management building all by himself in his black suit. Fancy that crazy Eyetie dressing up in his Sunday best, tie and all, to take over the works, like it was a wake or a wedding. Out he comes, ever so slow, walking and scratching his head, not with his hands up (why should he have his hands up?), and looking like he's thinking. He strolls forwards calm as you please, the first sparrows all around him chirping their heads off. But right there something drowns out the birds. There's this dry sound, rat-a-tat, rat-a-tat, you know? To begin with, I don't cotton on to what this noise is until I see Zanotti stop, lower the hand he's scratching his head with down to his stomach, clutching at it and beginning to fold up, in slow motion like, falling to his knees and then dropping head first. It's like he wanted to go to sleep, face down, stretched out, not moving a muscle. Then them sparrows start up again, and I'm staring at the little Eyetie there on the ground in his black funeral or wedding suit. Think a minute, now. If you see what I'm driving at, you'll see why I run out with me hands up, really up, shouting hold it, stop, stop.

You're thinking what a shitty coward, ain't you? A traitor, right?

But you've got a nipper, don't you? Then if you've got a kiddie, maybe you'll understand ...

[91]

THE LETTER
TO RICARDO

Liliana Heer

The letter to Ricardo, rubber-stamped 'No Return Address', came into the hands of an employee in Department 27 of the Office of Post and Telecommunications. The file on this employee notes his facial features, vital statistics, attire, fingerprints, and a particular tendency to apprise himself of the contents of the mails. This last word, even out of context, induced in him a state of ecstasy that resulted in his committing acts of gross moral turpitude.

Owing to the fact that the internal structure of the organization makes no disciplinary provision for crimes committed visually, in ensuing managerial meetings the employee was transferred from department to department until a position was found for him where his practice not only did not constitute eccentric behaviour but was consolidated into that of bearer of postal information and intelligence under the classification 'Secret'.

A number of assumptions were made concerning letters without a return address; first, that they were from persons who, owing to cumulative ignorance, failed to include the particulars of their name and address; second, that they were from persons so anxious to conclude their business that they posted their missives while in a state of oblivion brought on by total absorption in what they had just consigned to the letter-box; third, that they came from genuine cases, for which elaborate inspection procedures were set up, initiated by the aforementioned office. In accordance with the provisions of the law, the underhand conduct of these persons makes them liable to arbitrary punishment. As with all third categories, there were several further divisions. These in turn involved degrees of gravity of omission, classifiable under the following headings: amatory, anonymous, extortive, propagandistic, etc.

For four years Rubén had scrupulously read each item of the daily post, which he sorted into numbered boxes, except for correspondence touching on the erotic. This remained in brown canvas bags for a few months before being consigned to the basement, from where its subsequent destination is unknown.

It should surprise no one that our hero felt himself to be the proper recipient of this sub-group, since the duty of placing such letters in the bag fell to his hand, and by this act he became confused with the frustrated receiver.

In recent years, after a good deal of hesitation, he had ventured to misappropriate various letters, mostly from women who were no lovers of complaint but, on the contrary, harbouring traces of nostalgia for the secrecy that forced them to remain anonymous, were lavish in offers of themselves and in recollections of exquisite moments.

The letter to Ricardo upset him for an entire morning and prevented him from sorting his usual quota; that afternoon, still behind, he received comments from his superior, and these were repeated over the next few days, resulting after a given period in his dismissal.

Rubén ignored the warnings but, having retained every word of the outlandish syntax in his memory, in his overcoat pocket, and in his skin, he went on and on mumbling the convolutions of a story that was condensed into a few pages – a story he found incredible inasmuch as it constituted a paradigm of love.

About Ricardo, he was able to deduce a demonic face, periods of withdrawal, moments of clarity, his body outlined on top of the one who loved him, and his certainty of being loved even in the most complicated circumstances.

These things were invasive, and bit by bit they changed Rubén's habits until he was signing and answering to Ricardo's name.

About her, Rubén knew no more than her name. In his dreams, he recognized her on the apron of a stage or somewhere in the wings, her voice resounding like an echo.

THE VISITATION

Fernando Sorrentino

In 1965, when I was twenty-three, I was training as a teacher of Spanish language and literature. Very early one morning at the beginning of spring I was studying in my room in our fifth-floor flat in the only apartment building on the block.

Feeling just a bit lazy, every now and again I let my eyes stray beyond the window. I could see the street and, on the opposite side, old don Cesáreo's well-kept garden. His house stood on the corner of a site that formed an irregular pentagon.

Next to don Cesáreo's was a beautiful house belonging to the Bernasconis, a wonderful family who were always doing good and kindly things. They had three daughters, and I was in love with Adriana, the eldest. That was why from time to time I glanced at the opposite side of the street – more out of a sentimental habit than because I expected to see her at such an early hour.

As usual, don Cesáreo was tending and watering his beloved garden, which was divided from the street by a low iron fence and three stone steps.

The street was so deserted that my attention was forcibly drawn to a man who appeared on the next block, heading our way on the same side as the houses of don Cesáreo and the Bernasconis. How could I help but notice this man? He was a beggar or a tramp, a scarecrow draped in shreds and patches.

Bearded and thin, he wore a battered yellowish straw hat, and, despite the heat, was wrapped in a bedraggled greyish overcoat. He was carrying a huge, filthy bag, and I assumed it held the small coins and scraps of food he managed to beg.

I couldn't take my eyes off him. The tramp stopped in front of don Cesáreo's house and asked him something over the fence. Don Cesáreo was a bad-tempered old codger. Without replying, he waved the beggar away. But the beggar, in a voice too

low for me to hear, seemed insistent. Then I distinctly heard
don Cesáreo shout out, 'Clear off once and for all and stop
bothering me.'

The tramp, however, kept on, and even went up the three
steps and pushed open the iron gate a few inches. At this point,
losing the last shred of his small supply of patience, don Cesáreo
gave the man a shove. Slipping, the beggar grabbed at the fence
but missed it and fell to the ground. In that instant, his legs flew
up in the air, and I heard the sharp crack of his skull striking the
wet step.

Don Cesáreo ran on to the pavement, leaned over the beggar,
and felt his chest. Then, in a fright, he took the body by the feet
and dragged it to the kerb. After that he went into his house and
closed the door, convinced there had been no witnesses to his
accidental crime.

Only I had seen it. Soon a man came along and stopped by
the dead beggar. Then more and more people gathered, and at
last the police came. Putting the tramp in an ambulance, they
took him away.

That was it; the matter was never spoken of again.

For my part, I took care not to say a word. Maybe I was
wrong, but why should I tell on an old man who had never done
me any harm? After all, he hadn't intended to kill the tramp,
and it didn't seem right to me that a court case should embitter
the last years of don Cesáreo's life. The best thing, I thought,
was to leave him alone with his conscience.

Little by little I began to forget the episode, but every time I
saw don Cesáreo it felt strange to realize that he was unaware
that I was the only person in the world who knew his terrible
secret. From then on, for some reason I avoided him and never
dared speak to him again.

In 1969, when I was twenty-six, I was working as a teacher of
Spanish language and literature. Adriana Bernasconi had married not me but someone else who may not have loved and
deserved her as much as I.

At the time, Adriana, who was pregnant, was very nearly

due. She still lived in the same house, and every day she grew more beautiful. Very early one oppressive summer morning I found myself teaching a special class in grammar to some secondary-school children who were preparing for their exams and, as usual, from time to time I cast a rather melancholy glance across the road.

All at once my heart literally did a flip-flop, and I thought I was seeing things.

From exactly the same direction as four years before came the tramp don Cesáreo had killed – the same ragged clothes, the greyish overcoat, the battered straw hat, the filthy bag.

Forgetting my pupils, I rushed to the window. The tramp had begun to slow his step, as if he had reached his destination.

He's come back to life, I thought, and he's going to take revenge on don Cesáreo.

But the beggar passed the old man's gate and walked on. Stopping at Adriana Bernasconi's front door, he turned the knob and went inside.

'I'll be back in a moment,' I told my students and, half out of my mind with anxiety, I went down in the lift, dashed across the street, and burst into Adriana's house.

'Hello!' her mother said, standing by the door as if about to go out. 'What a surprise to see you here!'

She had never looked on me in anything but a kindly way. She embraced and kissed me, and I did not quite understand what was going on. Then it dawned on me that Adriana had just become a mother and that they were all beside themselves with excitement. What else could I do but shake hands with my victorious rival?

I did not know how to put it to him, and I wondered whether it might not be better to keep quiet. Then I hit on a compromise. Casually I said, 'As a matter of fact, I let myself in without ringing the bell because I thought I saw a tramp come in with a big dirty bag and I was afraid he meant to rob you.'

They all gaped at me. What tramp? What bag? Robbery? They had been in the living-room the whole time and had no idea what I was talking about.

'I must have made a mistake,' I said.

Then they invited me into the room where Adriana and her baby were. I never know what to say on these occasions. I congratulated her, I kissed her, I admired the baby, and I asked what they were going to name him. Gustavo, I was told, after his father; I would have preferred Fernando but I said nothing.

Back home I thought, That was the tramp old don Cesáreo killed, I'm sure of it. It's not revenge he's come back for but to be reborn as Adriana's son.

Two or three days later, however, this hypothesis struck me as ridiculous, and I put it out of my mind.

And would have forgotten it forever had something not come up in 1979 that brought it all back.

Having grown older and feeling less and less in control of things, I tried to focus my attention on a book I was reading beside the window, while letting my glance stray.

Gustavo, Adriana's son, was playing on the roof terrace of their house. Surely, at his age, the game he was playing was rather infantile, and I felt that the boy had inherited his father's scant intelligence and that, had he been my son, he would certainly have found a less foolish way of amusing himself.

He had placed a line of empty tin cans on the parapet and was trying to knock them off by throwing stones at them from a distance of ten or twelve feet. Of course, nearly all the pebbles were falling down into don Cesáreo's garden next door. I could see that the old man, who wasn't there just then, would work himself into a fit the moment he found that some of his flowers had been damaged.

At that very instant, don Cesáreo came out into the garden. He was, in point of fact, extremely old and he shuffled along putting one foot very carefully in front of the other. Slowly, timidly, he made his way to the garden gate and prepared to go down the three steps to the pavement.

At the same time, Gustavo – who couldn't see the old man – at last managed to hit one of the tin cans, which, bouncing off two or three ledges as it went, fell with a clatter into don

Cesáreo's garden. Startled, don Cesáreo, who was half-way down the steps, made a sudden movement, slipped head over heels, and cracked his skull against the lowest step.

I took all this in, but the boy had not seen the old man nor had the old man seen the boy. For some reason, at that point Gustavo left the terrace. In a matter of seconds, a crowd of people surrounded don Cesáreo's body; an accidental fall, obviously, had been the cause of his death.

The next day I got up very early and immediately stationed myself at the window. In the pentagonal house, don Cesáreo's wake was in full swing. On the pavement out in front, a small knot of people stood smoking and talking.

A moment later, in disgust and dismay, they drew aside when a beggar came out of Adriana Bernasconi's house, again dressed in rags, overcoat, straw hat, and carrying a bag. He made his way through the circle of bystanders and slowly vanished into the distance the same way he had come from twice before.

At midday, sadly but with no surprise, I learned that Gustavo's bed had been found empty that morning. The whole Bernasconi family launched a forlorn search, which, to this day, they continue in obstinate hope. I never had the courage to tell them to call it off.

A MEMORY OF PUNKAL

Angel Bonomini

I arrived in Punkal on an empty train. As far as I could tell, I was the only passenger on the whole three-hundred-mile journey. Several times during the trip, for no apparent reason, the train stopped; they were gloomy, pointless stops, since no one got on or off at these deserted stations.

My own repeated forays up and down the carriages in search of other passengers, or at least of a guard who might want to see my ticket or my passport, were also fruitless. Since the train had to cross the border and the customs office was the second stop, I assumed that this would probably be where I would have to show my papers and, as it were, establish that my trip was in order. I was no stowaway, after all, nor was I hiding anything; I was only trying to get to Punkal. But nothing happened. I noticed no one on any of the stations – neither passenger nor railwayman.

During the third and last scheduled stop before my destination, I admit that I behaved like a lunatic. I went down the three carriage steps and, hanging on to the handrail, I shouted that I was going to Punkal. Was there no one around, I asked angrily, no railway official even, to help passengers in the event of an emergency? I was shouting into the air, a cold night air, and the only reply was the engine's whistle. I climbed back into the carriage, and the doors slammed shut. I made one last if not very hopeful search, for – giving in to the grim reality of the situation – it suddenly struck me that I might have got on the wrong train. To some extent, my horror gave way to resignation.

It occurred to me that this train might be going to Punkal, the final stop on the line, for the sole purpose of picking up passengers there. If that were the case, I asked myself, what was the meaning of the last three stops; and in the end I decided it must have been a 'test run', a technical term that to me always conceals unfathomable mysteries but that in this case I connected with speed, wear and tear on the wheels and track, the amount of electricity consumed per mile, and the indispensable checking of the strict timetables we all marvel at and of course demand be adhered to, as if the price of the ticket included an absolute guarantee against the innumerable contingencies that may arise on a journey of several hundred miles.

The train at last entered a stretch of industrial suburbs, where it slowed to a walking pace. Then it halted for a minute or two, unloosing a wave of panic in me, after which it slowly ground on again.

It stopped in Punkal. I breathed a sigh of relief when I saw the signs with the city's name. Granted it was two in the morning and one hardly expected crowds, yet strange to say I saw no one in the station. I alighted with my suitcase and walked along the empty platform. The double-vaulted roof was supported by iron arches on concrete footings. Everything was solid, on a monumental scale, and, although the light in the vast, high-ceilinged hall was dim, here and there in the marble paving you could see incomprehensible symbols. Stone stairs led up from a lower hall, also marble-paved, bearing more indecipherable symbols. I made my way out into the street, where I felt better, and the fog – a soft bluish-grey fog – veiled the buildings and the skeletal trees on that mild, serene but implacably lonely autumn night.

The city was illuminated, though with a faint, shadowy light. I headed for the hotel where a room had been booked for me. Along the way, the architecture I saw was of various periods and styles, yet as diverse or remote as these were the city still maintained a clear unity. Buildings were endowed with a strange eloquence, with an obvious meaning quite different from that of those architectural styles in which silence, sobriety, and an absence of decorative or sculptural elements prevail. The coherence I noted derived from roundness and volume. The stone and marble, the solid iron grillwork, the imposing bronze gates and even the heavy wooden ones attested not so much to a defiance of time as to a disposition – one might almost say a deliberate intention – to negate it.

I reached the hotel; behind the sumptuous reception desk, with its switchboard and array of telephones, no one was in attendance. As my luggage was labelled with my name and I had no intention of going to bed just then, I left my case behind the counter with a note to the staff asking them to take the bag to Room 77 – the one reserved for me – and saying that I would return in an hour or two. Checking that I had my papers on me, I went back out into the street.

After turning down the Via della Campana, I came to Via Monte Emilia. Here there was more light. I breathed in deeply, for, despite the fact that there were no trees anywhere about, the air was heavily scented, and before I knew it I was brought up short by a shop window some fifteen feet long and three feet high. I have never had the slightest interest in jewels; of all objects of desire they are the ones whose capacity to fire the passions I least understand. In fact, as far as I can remember, no jewel ever interested me as much as a piece of driftwood or some bone picked up on a beach. Financial considerations aside, I would choose the feathers of certain birds over even an exquisite ring. Nevertheless, this beautiful window, glittering with watches, necklaces, and brooches, gave me a new appreciation of a world that had always been alien to me. Put another way, this display (which normally would have been of little interest to me) filled me with an irresistible desire to possess what it contained.

I noticed that the watches had stopped at different times. I looked at my own watch, which was of an undistinguished make, and its humbleness endeared it to me; all it had in common with the ones in the window was that it too had stopped – in its case, at the moment the train had arrived in Punkal.

There followed a whole series of shop windows. Each awakened a new desire, a new delight, a new craving for possession that somehow blinded judgement and common sense. One wanted everything, and everything seemed to advertise that it was, above all else, available. Furniture, jewels, furs, cars, clothes, fabrics – all tempted, and one felt that, whatever their price, they were in some way within reach. In other words, money was no longer the accepted tender but simply another commodity, which one had no need of here. As well as luxury goods, there were on display superb books, important paintings, and Greek, Etruscan, Roman and pre-Columbian works of art. As an art restorer, I have travelled in the course of my painstaking work from Lima to Florence, from London to Mexico, from Bogotá to Amsterdam, and I have to confess that the objects in the shop windows of Punkal were of a quality rare even in the greatest museums.

For a moment I stood dumbfounded. Steeped in Punkal's exquisite scents, I felt that this was a city of matchless perfection – so much so that I was even compelled to question my initial opinion of its architecture. Though I had no taste for the baroque nor for anything resembling it, I told myself I should have to rethink my over-hasty dismissal. The quality of this architecture had to be equal to everything else on display in this city, which was a veritable anthology of excellence.

Turning down a narrow street, I found another row of remarkable shop windows, where, instead of mannequins, ancient marble torsos were used to show off silks and furs. This struck me as sacrilegious. Still, the furs and silks, of excellent quality and impeccably matched colours, draped the magnificent sculptures so aesthetically that it was impossible to remain unimpressed.

At one street corner the perfume I had thought emanated from the walls began to fade, and there before me I came upon a sight utterly repellent to the human eye. It was a formless heap of corpses. I shuddered in horror and made to flee, but all at once my dismay abated and, as if wishing to detect a mistake or verify a fact, I drew closer and made certain that what I was seeing was no hallucination.

The fact was that immediately after this ghastly spectacle and the flicker of fear it generated, I went back to my window-shopping as if nothing had happened. But making my way along three or four more streets, I came across other corpses piled up in rigid contortions. Once again I felt the terror, but after a few steps again came ominous oblivion.

There was a shameful logic in all this. First the obvious horror, then the sham fear, then the cynical familiarity that turned into acceptance or a sort of calm oblivion – as if at the suspension of moral judgement memory refused to function, thereby changing the whole past into a cloud of emptiness. In the city of Punkal, it seemed that reality existed only in terms of the present; this was a fiendish negation of time, for to omit memory is to abolish the past and to deny the past is also to deny the future.

All this merchandise in the shops, it seems to me, played a singular role. I could be wrong – this may be no more than a subjective observation – but I shall repeat what I think I have already said or implied, which is that everything was readily available not in exchange for money but through a surrender of something clearly personal that I cannot exactly put a finger on but that was my own and that I was free to give or withhold.

This was how it worked: memory operated in a strange way. Those troughs of shame represented by the abandoned corpses were at once suppressed at the first shop window, which completely took over and held the interest and attention of the sole onlooker – in this instance, me. Furthermore, the horrific stench was quickly replaced by curtains of the most exquisite perfumes which, I was to discover, emanated at regular intervals from tiny holes at the metal bases of the shop windows and periodically enveloped me like gusts wafting from an invisible garden. The whole of Punkal was pervaded with the most delicious scent, so that these sudden islands of abominable stenches were disgusting enclaves in the midst of rich fragrance.

The horror was too present to be thought shocking. It had lost its uniqueness and become one of the city's everyday features. Passing by the unforgivable sights on those street corners was like passing through one of those dreams that you emerge from – however hideous it may have been – almost as if nothing had happened.

The fog came down and although it filled the streets with a soft translucency, it could not compete with the light in the shop windows. I heard the music of a barrel-organ, playing over and over again like that of a merry-go-round, and the longing for some living human face led me towards the place it seemed to come from. I kept hearing it closer and closer, then suddenly it ceased, and I slowed down so as to remain within earshot, and when it began again I quickened my step to reach it sooner. But however many times I seemed to be on the exact spot it was coming from I never got to it. Resigned to this, for a long time I stopped hearing it, but then it began again far away, growing nearer and nearer, until it seemed to be coming from me. Once more it retreated, shifting as if it came from a different source both within me and without. In this way the music came and went, fading and swelling as if on a fluctuating wind.

I sat down on the pavement, my back against a shop window, facing one of those gruesome sights. I felt I had to. To forget the horror was a kind of cowardice. I confirmed that the mere act of looking at something so extreme sapped my critical judgement and damped any vestige of feeling. My eyes came to rest on an arm that stuck out of the shapeless pile of corpses deposited there, I imagined – like so much rubble – by dump trucks. I looked at the arm with particular interest, for on its wrist was a watch like mine. I got up and slowly approached the heaped bodies. The man's head was turned away. Knowing exactly what was going to happen, I gently shifted his face towards me. Deep down inside, I knew I was going to find my own corpse amongst these remains. I must admit that a certain serenity, a certain peace, drained from my face. I saw part of my chest and that arm. On top and underneath me, the other bodies hid or showed their grey faces.

This discovery did not make me begin to think of myself as a wraith or a restless spectre or a phantom. On the contrary, I was still myself, with all the attributes of normal existence, like anyone who, looking at his hands, knows full well that those hands are his.

But in Punkal, despite these simple tests that assure us that we are alive, I also knew I was dead. This was not just an anticipation of what would one day unfailingly take place but something that in some concrete way had already happened. I did not see this duality as either metaphor or dream; I was dead and I was alive. There were, if you like, two simultaneous and parallel realities – that of my death and that of my existence. I was two, or, rather, one in two opposite states, neither of which was contradictory or exclusive. I had two real realities. All that had happened to me since boarding the train that brought me to Punkal my corpse could have recounted had its state not made such an act impossible. I can recount it because this dual condition of mine allows me a remnant of temporality, even though my state is scarcely different from that of my bloodless body, whose face is not entirely without peace and calm.

I realized that for one part of me – if I may put it this way – time had taken on a final serenity, while for the part walking about the streets of Punkal time revealed itself in a series of fitful presents, fragments of time, as if both eternity and temporality were imperfect or defective.

I thought I had found at least a clue to what had happened, when it struck me that this night in Punkal would never change, would never dissolve into dawn and a new day. On the other hand, I had no doubt that the moment would come when I would be summoned to a new parting on an empty train to another city, and I did not discount the likelihood that this would happen to me again and again.

The knowledge that I now feel neither sleepy nor hungry has helped me dismiss the notion of myself I had in Buenos Aires, where I thought I was a single whole and full of life when in fact that life was merely separation from the dead man, the scarcely imagined shade I never knew existed. This slender hypothesis,

I believe, arose from my conviction that Punkal is not the only city through which I will have to pass.

Returning to the pavement and sitting down again in the same place, I suddenly heard the chords of a guitar, and then a sweet, simple air. Whoever was playing this music knew how to beguile, but I did not set out to look for him, since I would not find him.

After some thought, I have concluded that I was not the only one in Punkal with two separate realities. All of those thrown in heaps on the street corners had this same duality. I was alone in this city, but we were all of us alone and did not see each other; all of us were wandering through these streets where the only things to be seen were man's greatest creations and death. The guitarist too, of course, was dead.

After some thought, I have reached the conclusion that my train had been full of passengers I could not see. We all arrived at Punkal as if at a stage of our journey. Somehow we shall be told when to go back to the station and take another empty train.

Those of us seeking or awaiting our ultimate deaths here in Punkal must suppress the fragile link that we still have with time and that gives us a twofold nostalgia – one for the world, the irrecoverable world of days and love, and the other for this newly perceived world marked by the unalterable peace of eternity.

For my own death to be complete, I must forget Buenos Aires and Punkal and any other cities I pass through, of which there remain only ashes in the recesses of my memory and imagination. Everything will have to be wiped clean, once and for all.

After some thought, I have also reached the conclusion that we shall have to know other cities, perhaps more fearful than this one, and then, when we have exhausted the necessary stages of darkness, a train in which each of us believes himself the only passenger will take us to the last station, the station of the unnameable city.

MULE

Jorge Asís

To Eduardo Galeano

With the hesitant manner that marks a traveller, the salesman got off the bus in the Andean village of Volpe. He stretched, took a pace or two, and caught the stare of a boy unloading luggage.

'Mule!' exclaimed the urchin.

Another lad (who was having scant luck in his trade as shoeshine boy) also stared, a strange blend of amazement and fear in his eyes.

The salesman (who had come to Volpe to sell pictures of Our Lord Jesus Christ) was baffled.

'Mule.'

Gripping his small suitcase, the salesman set off along the one street in Volpe that had a name.

Dust, sun, forlornness.

My God, said the God salesman to himself, who am I going to sell pictures of Christ to here?

He saw a bedraggled woman, who said, 'It's Mule,' then ducked back into her hovel.

A string of urchins gaped and began to follow at a distance; every now and again, one would come right up to him; others were called or grabbed by their mothers and dragged off home.

At every window the salesman saw eyes and, first here, then there, he heard:

'Mule.'

'Mule's back.'

'Mule's dead.' This one was a feeble old voice.

'No, it's Mule.'

'He's just like him, he is.'

'Look. It's him all right.'

'It is.'

'Daft, they're all daft.' Again the old, deathly voice.

[117]

A bit taken aback, but not caring much, the salesman looked around for what would doubtless be the village's sole boarding-house, which had to be close by.

Everything in this village must be close by, he thought, except God.

'The boarding-house?' he asked an old man, who, trembling and avoiding the salesman's eyes, pointed down the street.

His feet raised more dust, and as he went along windows and doors closed and opened.

My God, he said to himself, this village not only doesn't know God. It's far worse, these people don't even deserve to know God.

At the far end of the street he spotted a dismal wooden sign on which, in clumsy, almost defunct letters, it was still possible to read:

DON LUNA

ROOM & BOARD

DRINKS

Setting his case down on the ground for a moment, the salesman clapped his hands. From a verandah of potted plants and darkness and cobwebs appeared a dark-haired, barefoot woman with fat, shapeless, puckered legs. She held a bucket in her hand and, opening her eyes impossibly wide, she said:

'Mule!'

And she dropped the bucket; in moments the ground (which was thirstier than the salesman) drank up all the water.

'Mule died thirty-five days ago, sir.

'He looked just like you, really. Same beard, maybe a little longer, but just as black.

'Though from close up your eyebrows are more arched. It's only a small detail. And Mule may have been half an inch taller, not more.

'Now take eating. You're not at all alike there. Mule ate – how can I put it? – a lot faster than you, more hungrily. I don't know, am I making myself clear?

Mule

'Up close your hair is different. Mule never combed his hair, whereas yours has a style, you know what I mean? Your hair may not be combed just now, but it has a style. You comb your hair sometimes, don't you?'

The salesman said he did.

'Not Mule. Mule's hair was completely wild.

'He was very kind – to everyone.

'I can't get over it, sir, how you're the dead spit of him. It's a good thing they took Concepción away to Chamical.'

Listening, the salesman ate.

Don Luna, the proprietor of the boarding-house, was also the mayor of Volpe and the only one who believed that the salesman wasn't Mule, that they were lookalikes and that's all, so why get so excited? Luckily, don Luna believed the man was a salesman of pictures of Our Lord Jesus Christ and a stranger in these parts. That's who he was, not Mule.

'A pity,' said don Luna.

By now the salesman knew that he would waste his time in Volpe, that he would sell nothing. In which case, he might as well leave.

Because these people don't know God, he ruminated with a touch of exaggeration as he ate and don Luna went on talking about how alike he and Mule were.

He would have a good long sleep in Volpe, and that night, when the bus passed through, he'd make his getaway to some other town, any town, where he'd be more likely to sell his Jesus Christs.

I hope I have more luck; I need it, he thought.

In Volpe, as the mayor himself had already told him, nobody worked.

'What at, sir, what at?

'See how we live.

'Have you a family to take a child off to?

'Take one.

'We have two or three pregnant woman just now, and they're very young. If you like, wait a few months and take the babies.

'Free – take them.'

The salesman was aware of a group of people standing in the doorway.

A murmuring, a shout or two, a greeting, the word Mule.

Time and again, don Luna had gone out to speak to them, to tell them that they were wrong and that they should go home, because though the visitor was a lot like Mule in fact he wasn't.

'Why should I hide him from you if he's Mule? But he isn't. Now clear off.'

When he came back to the table, where the salesman was eating with daunting slowness, the mayor said:

'They don't believe me, sir.'

'You have no idea how much we loved Mule, sir.

'They call me don Lunar. Because of my last name and because of this *lunar*, this mole, I have here, see.

'His was the most mourned death in the village – the children, the few young people still here, the old people.

'You must understand them. It's uncanny how like him you are.

'Just now you made a face exactly like Mule used to. You may think I'm lying, but you even have the same stare. Your smile must be exactly like his too, I imagine, even though I've never seen you smile.'

Finishing a slow, greasy, tasteless soup, the salesman asked don Luna why they called him Mule and how old he was when he died.

'Twenty-seven, sir.

'He was one of the few young men of that age living in the village. That is to say, who was normal. Because there's Acuña's son, but he's been a dimwit from the day he was born, poor thing. And Peláez' boy, but with him it's because he has no legs. He had an accident, poor lad. A bus ran him over on the highway. For, as you ought to be aware, as soon as they reach sixteen or seventeen the boys up and leave. Some even earlier. They're right; I'd do the same myself. What's there for them here?'

'Mule, come on out,' they were shouting from the door.

'They head for the cities, Buenos Aires even, where they can get work – where at least there's a chance of finding work, I don't say getting it. And as they're not choosy they find it. The girls get live-in jobs as housemaids. There are dozens of girls from Volpe working in Buenos Aires, dozens. They only come back for Carnival, and when they come they take away other girls, and so it goes on.

'But not Mule. Mule never wanted to leave Volpe. He said he was from here, that this was his place. He said he wanted to die here. Poor lad, he was in love with his own little corner.

'Excuse me for asking and don't get me wrong, but how old are you?'

'Twenty-eight,' replied the salesman.

'You still haven't told me why he was called Mule.'

'So I haven't. Even the dogs wept for Mule. And after he died, Concepción, his wife, went back to live with her parents. She tried to kill herself several times – five or so. That's why about a week ago her parents took her to Chamical – because there in Chamical they have relatives who are well off, they have room, they were able to take her in. And that's what they did. Poor girl, and poor parents too, what a cross. People say they had to watch her day and night so that she didn't get hold of a knife. She tried to kill herself with all sorts of things. People say they had to mind everything – knives, razor blades, detergents, and poison. People say she can't live without Mule. It's worse than hard, it's impossible. People say Mule meant the world to her.

'Each time the Angelus began to ring she'd go to the cemetery, and she'd stay by Mule's grave a long, long time, whether the day was hot or cold. Even when it was windy, she loved him so much.

'Her parents loved him too. They're honest people, salt of the earth. The man wore himself out working wherever he could, doing any work he could get. He'd go off at harvest time and stay away at least a year – or more. He worked on the bridges too. Good, honest people, as I was telling you, and they were afraid.

'So, seeing exactly how afraid they were, they gave a handful of coins to the youngest Oliveira boy, asking him to hide in the cemetery and watch what their daughter did, since she always insisted on going there alone and never wanted anyone with her, not even her mother.

'They were afraid, very afraid, because Concepción is all they have in the world. They were afraid she'd do something mad. Taking her away was the right thing.

'Hidden among the graves, the Oliveira boy kept an eye on her and he said Concepción talked to Mule.

'Her parents were even more scared when the lad told them she spoke to Mule as if he weren't dead. They thought Concepción might go mad again, clear out of her mind, and that's why they took her to Chamical. They did the best thing.

'The boy said a lot of what she said he couldn't understand, and he's a bright lad. He said sometimes Concepción would laugh and say she loved Mule very much and was waiting for him and she'd keep on waiting because she knew he wasn't dead and a whole lot of other things that the boy didn't understand.

'Three times he went spying on her, and he said he didn't want to any more because it frightened him, and he's quite a brave lad, sir. Oliveira, his father, didn't want him to go any more either and he asked don Pardo, Concepción's father, to forgive him but his son wasn't going to go any more. Oliveira said ever since the boy had been spying in the cemetery he'd been off colour, strange, and unable to sleep, and when he did he'd sometimes cry out.

'That was why they took Concepción Pardo to Chamical to stay with relatives. I hope it's for the best and that she'll get better.'

'Come on out, Mule!' the God salesman clearly heard.

He lit a cigarette and poured himself more wine.

He felt tired, strange.

'Why did they call him Mule?'

Don Luna burst out laughing. He had barely three teeth in his mouth, all of them rotten.

'They called Paulo Mule because of the way he kicked when he played football. His shots at goal were so powerful nobody could get near them. Cannon blasts they were.

'They called him Mule for another reason too – because of the kicks he dealt his opponents when he played in the defence.

'We also called him Mule for the punch he packed. He could throw a hard punch, but don't think Mule was a brawler. He'd take a lot of provocation before he'd fight. But let me tell you, anyone he fought with, it was good-bye. Whenever some bully boy tried to pick a fight with one of the smaller lads, Mule would wade in, and good-bye. And if he ever saw anything unfair, something that just wasn't on or that seemed that way to him, he'd wade right in, and good-bye.

'Gangs of louts from nearby towns, Lezamo, Fisgot, sometimes came to Volpe just to provoke him. You should have seen him – Mule acting like a mule. That's another reason why we called him Mule, because of the way he so easily turned mulish whenever he felt like it. When they saw Mule wasn't reacting, the louts swaggered and crowed, thinking Mule was cowering, that he had no guts.

'Poor them.

'After a while, when he was goaded beyond bearing, Mule laid into them, leaving them half senseless.'

'Come out, Mule.'

'Mule, we love you; come on out.'

Don Luna wiped his eyes with a handkerchief.

'We all loved him, sir. Forgive me,' said don Luna, for he was crying, and the salesman had noticed.

But what the salesman did not understand was don Luna's sudden snort of laughter, laughter amidst tears. He tried to explain, but the snort was stronger, and he couldn't.

'We also called him Mule,' he said when he had stopped laughing, 'because of the huge pizzle between his legs. It was a real mule's pizzle.'

For the first time in Volpe, the salesman smiled.

'Yes, just as I thought, even your smile's the same, the very same.

'Ah, but how Mule played football, sir. He taught the boys how to control the ball in mid-air with their chests, to feint and swerve, to dribble and pass with the inside of the foot.

'It was a pity Concepción never gave him a child, because he was so fond of the village boys.

'Oh, yes, he also taught them to keep their heads up when attacking. To face forwards, always looking where they were about to send the ball.'

'Come on out, Mule.'

The God salesman poured himself another glass of wine, while once again don Luna went out to try to control the crowd.

But it was no use trying to convince them. They didn't believe him.

Juana, the mother of Cosme the epileptic, told don Luna he must have hidden him.

What was worse, don Luna found out that Concepción's cousin Vargas had set off for Chamical to tell her Mule had come back.

When don Luna returned the salesman was no longer there but had gone to lie down for his afternoon nap. So, all on his own, don Luna sat down, poured himself a glass of wine, propped his elbows on the table, and, face in his hands, remembered all about the tall, burly, bearded, rugged, unkempt young man calling to him from the street, smiling, in a hurry:

'So long, don Lunar.

'It's a good life, don Lunar.'

Don Luna smiled now, his elbows on the table, remembering. But when he looked towards the door, his smile vanished. The whole population of the town was waiting for Mule to come out.

'Fools,' he shouted, 'Mule's dead.'

'You're lying!'

'Dead, do you hear, dead.' Don Luna probably did not realize he was crying.

'He's in there; bring him out,' shouted Osorio.

'Bring him out, otherwise we'll fetch him by force,' and the mayor had no trouble recognizing old Lemos's voice.

'We want to see him.' This time it was a woman's voice – Márquez'.

'Don't be stupid; he's dead,' shouted don Luna.

'Mooley, Mooley,' shouted Acuña's son, the village simpleton.

'Mooley.'

The salesman guessed at, listened to, wondered about the noise. He was finding it harder than ever to enter the antechamber of sleep. Because he never had much on his mind, he was lucky and usually he fell asleep at once. That was before today.

Before today, whenever he lay down to sleep and sleep didn't want to come, he would think about the instalments due on the Our Lord Jesus Christ pictures. Whether a customer had got together enough money for the first payment. Whether they might be able to pay the whole sum cash on delivery. Yes, he was happy when he sold a Jesus Christ for cash. He would also think (before today, whenever he couldn't sleep) about whether money orders would be paid on time, because they might not, and if they weren't the danger was that the customer would have spent the money saved up for the first instalment, maybe on bread, in which case there'd be even less likelihood of his handing over God for ready money.

Before today, the God salesman used to think about the difficulties he'd had in making a sale to an atheist. To send himself to sleep he'd think about the effort he'd made, telling himself he was an outstanding salesman. Then he would remember his concentration on the holy words of the Bible and God will provide and the Testaments so as to help him sell a picture to that atheist. He remembered the ins and outs of the sales pitch he had to make to pressure people into buying the pictures of Our Lord Jesus Christ stupidly crucified.

'He died, he died for us,' he would say.

He remembered (before today, to send himself to sleep) the

most powerful, persuasive selling points – religious, financial, and financially religious points. For example, telling people, 'When we die ours will be the kingdom of heaven, and for a few pesos a month you can have in your own home something like this, like a little church.

'You too will become the representative of Our Lord here on earth, señora.'

He remembered knocking on doors, clapping his hands outside miserable huts, and touting his oval-framed pictures. Inside each frame, in plaster of Paris, the desolate image of a stupidly crucified Christ.

'He died for us,' he told the poor. 'We are guilty of his death. Ours will be the kingdom of heaven. He', he would say, pointing to the picture, 'has bequeathed us a message of love, of peace, a divine message of faith.

'And this, señora, this divine message of love, is within the reach of any budget. We can adjust ourselves to the budget of the faithful. How much can you pay monthly? Tell me.'

Despicable, thought the salesman when he couldn't sleep. When he told himself that, really, he was a cynic. A common scoundrel, a poor bastard who'd never believed a word of what he said. Still less in the existence of God, although he spent all day talking about him. Despicable, and he was a good salesman, he knew. From time to time, he justified himself by saying that the existence of God was a tax on his own existence. He knew that to sell God well to the faithful poor he had to convince himself of the truth of certain words he used. Despicable, because this meant he had to sell his words first, to believe in them, to convince himself in such a way that he turned himself into a buyer of God.

So, then, he had to buy something he didn't believe in, which meant he would never have the right to doubt, because then he wouldn't sell a single Christ and wouldn't be paying the tax on his existence. Despicable.

He knew perfectly well that when he went out into the streets to talk about the kingdom of heaven and about when we die, without being convinced either of the kingdom or of paradise when we die, he never sold a single Christ to anyone.

The first sale and the most difficult was selling God to himself. For ready cash. And by the time he had sold him to himself (or bought him) and he went out into the streets, all preacher now, he knew more verses by heart than a country priest. He spoke to the poor with great conviction, not only about the kingdom of heaven and God will provide but also about the crown of thorns, the widow's mite, and the commandments.

So all the salesman had to do was not to think, not to doubt, but to drink plenty of wine. And, the moment his head hit the pillow, sleep.

But during this siesta in the village of Volpe he couldn't get to sleep. He heard the shouts of the crowd, and this set him thinking. Most of all he thought about never having had anything to call his own, while Mule had had more than his share.

The salesman had never punched anyone. The salesman hadn't even learned to dribble a ball with the inside of his foot. The salesman had never had a woman close to suicide over him. So once more he thought about having lived by selling God without loving or believing in him. He thought about having landed in a sorry, out-of-the-way village so far from God that no one knew him. So for the first time he had to sell God, but with sincerity, as if the whole thing were true. But first and foremost, if he wanted to sleep he had to stop thinking, he had to let himself go.

'Don Luna,' he called out suddenly from his bed.

The mayor of Volpe came to the doorway. A thatched roof, deep gloom, flies.

'What did Mule die of?'

'They did him an injury,' don Luna said, reluctant.

Half asleep, the salesman turned over, longing to drop off.

Then at last the salesman slept.

He dreamed about the afternoon he hadn't headed a last-minute goal against Fisgot, making Volpe league champions.

He dreamed about the afternoon he hadn't defended don Peláez' son when some husky louts from Sayago tried to rough him up, mocking him, bullying him. Then he waded in, and good-bye.

He also dreamed about that siesta when he hadn't made love to Concepción for the first time, when he kissed her all over under cover of a stunted tree on the left-hand side of the road to Chepes. She was dark, her skin quite dusky, her eyes sparkled like the night.

He dreamed about a lot of things that he had never taken part in. He dreamed, for example, about teaching the village boys how to control a ball, how to bring a foot down on it, how to keep their heads up, especially when moving forwards. He dreamed about teaching them to hold their own when jumped from behind; he dreamed about teaching them knockout punches, blows that would flatten an elephant.

He dreamed about telling the other young men they should never leave the village. Because our place is here, and we have no business turning our backs on it. Because this is our land, and we've grown up here, loved here, suffered here. So it's our duty to make this land into a paradise. Because if it's true that we the poor have already gained the kingdom of heaven, then we must begin the struggle to gain the kingdom of this earth.

He dreamed about the young men listening to him but still going off to the cities to work for a pittance. The girls listened too, heeding him and some of them weeping, but still they went off to the cities to work for a pittance, to become housemaids, to return perhaps never or for Carnival.

He dreamed about telling them to no avail that all this is ours and nobody else's, that we don't need to go selling our unborn, we don't need to give them away. Stay here.

But all the same they went off to the cities to work for a pittance.

'Mule, come on out!'

He turned over and at once remembered the day he hadn't

suffered the injury that led to his death. An injury was too small a thing to kill Mule, but even if it was that that had killed him he must now be in the kingdom of heaven – of course, being poor. So he must be in heaven, and the kingdom of heaven just as on earth had a sorry, out-of-the-way village called Volpe, and Volpe is in heaven as it is on earth. In other words, all his life he had been cheated and had himself cheated in selling these stupid pictures of a Jesus Christ stupidly crucified because he died for us, because he died in very few, easily payable monthly instalments.

He turned over again and the kingdoms of heaven and earth got mixed up with the goal header he didn't score against Fisgot and the first kiss he didn't give Concepción under that stunted tree on the left-hand side of the road to Chepes.

Also, disagreeably, a door worked its way into his dream, opening reluctantly. A poor woman came out because a commercial traveller in God had clapped his hands. A commercial traveller in God who was showing her a picture of Our Lord Jesus Christ.

He died for us, so that we might have our daily bread. You, me. All of us are guilty of his death. But he bequeathed us a legacy of peace, of love, of faith. In easy monthly instalments, ours will be the kingdom of heaven. We should all have an altar of our own, in thanks to the Lord.

'Mule, come on out.'

'We love you, Mule.'

'Mooley,' said the simpleton.

Until the salesman woke up. He was shaking.

As soon as he got up he stopped trembling. He went to the verandah, saw the cobwebs, the potted plants, and heard the word Mule.

He came along the verandah, with don Luna staring at him from where he sat, elbows on the table, probably thinking what a pity.

'Good evening, don Lunar,' said the salesman.

The moment Mule came out into the street there was celebration. Everyone embraced him, he embraced them. There was laughter, tears, shouts, and even a death: don Luna had stayed right there where he was sitting, staring at him, but it was not until a few days later that they realized he was dead.

Some of them (don Lemos, for one) found that Mule's eyebrows were a bit more arched and that he was at least half an inch shorter, but it wasn't much.

That same night, her cousin Vargas turned up with Concepción. There she was, black hair, dark skin, her eyes open wide and sparkling like the day.

'Paulo,' she said from some way off.

And at once Mule recognized her.

While the villagers laughed, wept, drank wine, and went home happy because they had Mule back, the two of them clasped each other in desperation.

By the different warmth radiating from his embrace, Concepción soon realized that this was not the same Paulo. Yet they went walking along the path to Chepes, where, on the left-hand side, grew a stunted tree.

He kissed her like that first time, but after the kiss she pushed him away and went running off down the path.

Concepción was never again seen in Volpe.

When Mule went back to his football (to make things worse, it was against Fisgot) he didn't once pass, he didn't take a shot at goal, he never once got near the ball; in fact, he didn't see the ball at all. As if that were not enough, he missed a penalty. He fluffed an impossibly easy shot even though he was alone in front of an undefended goal.

To round it off, three Fisgot louts, the Ledesma brothers, turned on the youngest Oliveira boy, the one who had spied. They roughed him up, mocking and trying to bully him. The whole of Volpe stood watching Mule, because when Mule waded in, good-bye.

Surrounded by all those staring eyes, Mule made up his mind to take the trio on. He barely managed a feeble jab at the burliest Ledesma. But the half-pint brother, the froth of the three, caught Mule a blow to the stomach, right in the solar plexus.

Then, while he was doubled over, the smallest Ledesma hit him again, this time on the jaw. There was no need for more, because Mule was already out cold on the ground, arms spread, feet together, blood in his beard, and good-bye.

FOR
SERVICES RENDERED

Abelardo Castillo

His nickname stemmed from an inability to tell his left foot from his right and from the perverse sense of humour of the commander of the second company, Captain Losa, with whom he was now trapped in a crevasse on a by-way off the Zapala road. Juan Alfonso was his name, Alfonso, his surname. How or why he'd been allowed to join up, no one was quite sure. The fact was that he had.

He showed up one morning to enlist, either that or was brought in by force from his hut in the mountains. And, as if waiting for something, he remained for three years. He did no harm to anyone, and they let him stay. Feeding and watering the company mules, with which he sometimes slept, sweeping out the barracks, and whistling were the only things he appeared to have a knack for. To watch him eating troops' rations was a comic, almost revolting, sight. He ate without lifting his head from his plate, like a child or a caged animal, peering at his comrades out of the corner of his eye as if any one of them might prove a secret enemy – or momentary brother – likely to squabble over those unspeakable slops.

Pasto Seco, Dry Grass, was his nickname. One night, three years earlier, Captain Alvaro Losa, who had been transferred to that border outpost for disciplinary reasons, although no one knew why or from where, ordered Alfonso to tie a handful of dry grass to his left buskin and another of green grass to his right. Getting the duty quartermaster to brew him some maté, the captain made Alfonso march up and down the barracks to the command 'Dry, green; dry, green', in front of the whole second company, shivering in their underwear at the foot of their beds.

And now here were the two of them, trapped together at the bottom of an abyss more than twelve feet deep, somewhere along one of the by-roads up from Zapala, assuming that their compass was really pointing north after the captain's horse trod on it and before they lost both compass and horse when they fell into the crevasse. A sudden blizzard cutting them off from their reconnaissance party, they lost their way in the drifts, blundered on clinging together towards the abyss, there was an explosion above their heads, and Losa and Pastoseco found themselves trapped in the gully. There was something they could try, thinks Captain Losa. He looks at his watch, at Pastoseco's eyes, but dares not say anything.

The Indian had had this same look on his face since that night. For Pastoseco was an Indian, or half-Indian, a descendant of Pampa or Araucanian Indians – no one knew which. He'd had the nickname and the look since then, since the night of his solitary march up and down between the rows of beds, back and forth, back and forth, the whole company ranged on either side watching, and he tramping up and down with tufts of grass, one green, one dry, in each laced boot. Or maybe not the look, only the nickname. The look he had from before that, long before. It was colder than his eyes – that was the impression it gave. His big brown eyes were translucent, which is unusual for an Indian. In the irises were bright, greyish specks.

That was also the night Captain Losa had mentioned the orbs and pair of wings. It happened like this. On one of his to-ings and fro-ings, the Indian simply stopped. He just stood there, stock still, while Losa, who was looking the other way, went on bawling, 'Dry, green; dry, green,' for several seconds longer. But after a moment or two he couldn't help noticing the deathly hush in the barracks. Refusing the maté handed him by the quartermaster, the captain turned and looked at the Indian – at his back – for the Indian stood there, ten yards away, his back to Losa and absolutely still.

Losa leapt to his feet in disbelief, bellowed to the Indian to come to him, shouting, 'At the double,' and half unsheathed his sabre.

The Indian did not move.

'So,' said the captain, 'I'm the lucky sod in command of a

company of bloody-minded, pig-headed soldier boys, am I?'
Then, addressing them all, he added: 'Am I right?'

No one answered.

'Am I right or aren't I?'

'No, sir,' chorused the company.

Pensively, without looking at the Indian, the captain strode
down the row of beds, striking his boot rhythmically with the
flat of his now unsheathed sword. Thrusting out his bottom lip,
he shook his head as if lost in thought. Then he said, 'So it isn't
true?'

'No, sir,' replied the company.

'So it isn't, then?' Losa shouted. 'Do you mean to say I'm
lying, damn it? Everyone, double mark time!'

For ten minutes, the whole company, in their underwear, six
inches out from the foot of their beds, ran on the spot, each on
one square floor tile. Only Alfonso did not move. As if he'd had
trouble understanding, he just stood there in the middle of the
barracks. A deep groove, like a parting, furrowed his brow, and
his eyes had narrowed to slits.

'Attention!' shouted Losa. The captain was a big man, tall
and burly, and more than one recruit had seen him fell an
obstinate mule with a single blow between the eyes. Pastoseco
was on the scrawny side, and next to the other man he looked
like a child.

Too thin, thinks Losa in the crevasse, and, gazing up at the
sheer scarp, he sees Pastoseco's mule, which has followed them
through the blizzard, looking at them from on high with the
aloofness of an idol. Too thin, the captain thinks, he won't
support my weight. Scrawny was not the word. The Indian was
worn out. Not from marching up and down, but as if from ages
past, from the blood of his race, long since tame or tamed over
years of degradation and systematic extermination.

When Losa had drawn up to him, bellowing, 'Double march
to the end of the room,' his voice rang with such authority that a
number of the recruits made an instinctive move to run. The
Indian did not stir. For a moment, it was as if Losa and he were
the only people in the world, so great was the silence. Then,

unexpectedly, Losa calmed down. Rummaging in the breast pocket of his tunic, he pulled out a small silvery object, a sort of badge consisting of a pair of wings.

'Quartermaster,' he called.

The quartermaster came running up and stood to attention. 'Sir.'

'What's this?' asked Losa.

'A pair of wings, sir.'

'Speak up,' said Losa without raising his voice. 'I want everyone to hear.'

'A pair of wings,' cried the soldier.

'There's something else,' said Losa. 'Down here,' and he pointed to the lower edge of the wings. 'Look again, soldier boy.'

The quartermaster laughed and said nothing.

'Can't you see what's there?' asked Losa.

'Yes, sir,' the soldier called out, smiling.

And Losa told them what was there, all the while staring at the line of recruits who stood at the foot of their beds. It was a pair of balls. With wings. Not raising his voice, the captain repeated it several times. 'A pair of balls, and this little badge represents an allegory, an emblem. Does anyone know what an emblem is? It's a symbol,' he shouted. 'And what does that mean? It means that here, in my company, your balls stay locked up in my trunk all year.'

As he spoke he was pacing up and down, and when he finished his tirade he stood in front of the Indian, holding the wings up to him. 'In this company, anyone with balls flies.' Putting the pair of wings away, Losa ordered, 'Hit the ground,' and with the inside edge of his boot he kicked the Indian on the shin, and the Indian slumped, skidded a yard or two over the tiled floor, and fell flat, never once taking his eyes off the captain, staring at him out of those odd-coloured eyes with their tiny, icy stars around the pupils.

And now in the crevasse, in spite of himself, Losa recalls the Indian's look, remembers crouching there beside him, shouting, 'Double march,' surprised by the stony submissiveness of those eyes, sorry for the Indian, but for a split second their faces were so near that Losa saw the cold tints in the Indian's irises and he feared that Pastoseco might not obey his next order. 'To the end of the room, double march,' the captain had shouted, trying to stare the Indian down, but in the end, imperceptibly, he averted his eyes from that look, which here in the crevasse blends into this one, because they are one and the same.

Above them, the mule comes in sight again. Losa thinks that there is, in any case, only one way out but he cannot bring himself to suggest that the Indian clamber up on his shoulders. He might make off on his own, Losa thinks. Three years before, one hundred soldiers in their underwear had bet that the Indian would refuse to obey him, and Losa had seen that his whole authority depended on whether the Indian obeyed or turned and struck him. Losa gave the order just once. And the Indian, who for a moment or two looked as if he was going to do something else, got to his feet, ran to the far end of the barracks – back and forth, back and forth, in time to Losa's commands, losing his cap, scattering grass in all directions, crawling on all fours – and, in the end, just sat there on the floor, gasping, 'Enough, captain, sir,' to the cheers of the hundred recruits and the guffaws of the captain, Alvaro Wenceslao del Sagrado Corazón Losa himself, who this time told the Indian, 'All right, but before you go to bed I want you to give the barracks a good sweeping,' and who now is here in the crevasse with the Indian, huddled up to and almost hugging him, and who has just decided that if within the hour no rescue party turns up he's going to have to get out somehow. Or else, he thinks, tonight, when the reconnaissance party gets back to the post, there'll be one officer, his horse, and one mule less. Assuming anything remains of the reconnaissance party. And within a week, if there was anyone left to notify the garrison, his wife was going to receive a telegram from the Nation. Missing in the line of duty. Promoted to major for services rendered. So frozen solid that they're going to have to bury us in the same box, he thinks, thinking about the Indian for the first time. That way, Pastoseco may even be made corporal.

Losa studies at length the twelve-foot drop above their heads. It was on that night three years before that the Indian had received his nickname and become the second company's most envied recruit, because from that night on and, more specifically, as a result of that act of sitting there on the barracks floor, gasping for breath and calling Losa 'captain, sir', Losa, of whom they told stories of mules felled by a single blow to the centre of the forehead, from that act or those words on – or perhaps because of that bond that grows imperceptibly between vanquisher and vanquished, between the whipped animal and the man who tames it – the captain went nowhere without the Indian. And he made him his assistant.

'My lieutenant,' he would say, clapping the Indian on the back, or he'd say, 'My boots, Pastoseco,' and the Indian would polish them with painstaking, almost ceremonial, dedication, but without servility and perhaps without concern, just as snow falls or as things happen in nature. And the odd thing is that Losa never made him polish his boots when he was wearing them, nor did he order the Indian to take them off or put them on him – or maybe there had been a first time, when the Araucanian decided that such things were not part of the natural order.

Forty-five minutes, thinks Losa, and again he gazes up at the scarp above their heads. The Indian has begun to whistle. Twelve feet, maybe thirteen, thinks Losa. The rest is not hard to work out. Even supposing that Pastoseco could support on his shoulders the captain's two hundred and twenty pounds (he's much too small, Losa thinks), the lip of the crevasse would still be a good ten or twelve inches out of reach, and after that – and this went without saying – not even two Indians like this one would have the strength in their wrists to raise him to the edge.

'Come here,' says Losa. 'Climb up here.'

He gets on his knees, holds his hands up at shoulder level, and makes Pastoseco place his feet in them as if in stirrups.

'Try to reach the lip,' Losa says.

He raises himself, slowly, with the Indian on top of him, his eyes fixed on the sheer wall above, taking care not to lose sight of Pastoseco's hands. When the Indian's hands are about to take hold of the lip, Losa suddenly drops to his knees again, lowering the Indian.

'It can be done,' says Pastoseco.

'Yes,' says Losa. 'It can be done.'

He looks at his watch and tells the Indian to come closer. The Indian sits crouching far away. Two yards is far away in a hole two yards long. Losa tells the Indian to come close or he'll freeze. He does not say we'll freeze. 'You'll freeze,' he says. 'Come near or you'll freeze, you dumb Indian. Your mule has a rope on it, doesn't it?' asks Losa. 'And a lance?'

'It does.'

'If one of us gets to the top,' says Losa, 'he can tie the rope to the mule's girth and throw the other end and the lance down here into the crevasse. Then the other can climb out.'

Pastoseco's face lights up. Something unusual comes over him, and he breaks into a loud laugh. It's the first time Losa has ever seen an Indian laugh like that.

'And if we don't, then what, captain, sir?' says the Indian.

In a moment or two, all that remains is his habitual gloom, the ghost of a smile on his stony face. He has closed his eyes, and Losa is afraid the Indian is asleep. If he falls asleep, he'll die, Losa thinks. And if I fall asleep, I'll die too.

He takes out his pistol and fires a shot into the air. The Indian does not open his eyes.

'I'm not asleep,' says the Indian, his eyes shut. 'And don't fire again or you'll bring everything down on us. All the snow. It's no good scaring the mule off, either.'

Distantly, the last echo of the shot can be heard. Then a growl of thunder, a low rumble that seems to grow nearer, sending tremors through the floor of the crevasse. Then nothing. Only the Indian's whistling.

Pastoseco had stayed on three years, just as he might have stayed on three hundred. He never stood sentry or night watch except during the week when Losa was on duty. The Indian came and went, whistling and brewing the captain endless maté.

Very early one morning, the recruit who slept in the first bed came into the duty room.

'What's the matter?' said Losa.

'I can't sleep, sir,' and he pointed at the Indian. 'It's his whistling.'

'What did you say your name was?' said Losa.

'Petrucelli, Omar,' said the soldier.

'Stuff it,' said Losa. 'And now that you're awake, get dressed, and brew the two of us some maté.'

Later, while Petrucelli was brewing maté, Losa said, 'This fellow here, Private Petruchoto, is a Pampa Indian, an Araucanian. Or what remains of the Araucanian. When Michelangelo was sucking up vermicelli on the scaffolding of the Sistine Chapel, that man's forefathers were beginning to fight mine. Three hundred years they fought each other. Us shooting the hell out of them, them spearing the hell out of us. Three hundred years it took us to bequeath them that dumb face. Before your lot had set foot on the pampa – '

'Calfucurá rode his horse down the main street of Bahía Blanca.' The Indian interrupted the captain, very softly, as if it were not an interruption.

Captain Losa looked at him. 'What did you say?'

'Things the old ones tell,' Pastoseco murmured.

'You mean to tell me you know who Calfucurá was?'

The Indian kept his eyes on his maté cup. 'He was an Indian,' he said.

'Finish your maté once and for all,' said Losa, 'and turn in, but before you do polish my boots.'

Pastoseco looked at Losa's buskins and then, without expression, stared the captain in the face.

'No, bloody hell,' said Losa, 'my riding boots – they're in my trunk. We'll have Umberto the First here polish the buskins. Do you know, Private Petrafofa, the only true Argentines in this country are a cross between this animal here and people like me. Don't take offence, soldier. Your lot's done its bit too.

That's why this country is a shambles. And that's why the zoo is in the Plaza Italia.'

And suddenly he turned to Pastoseco and barked, 'He rode his horse down the main street of Bahía, did he? Well, he almost rustled two hundred thousand head of cattle. And he died like an old rogue after the lesson we taught them at Bolívar – tell that to the aged cowpats of your tribe when you go back. If you go back. Ah, and don't skimp on the polish.'

The mule comes back to the edge of the crevasse again. The Indian, his eyes still shut, stops whistling and, out of the blue, says, 'Let me see the little wings.'

The other man looks at him seriously and with suspicion.

'What for?' says the captain.

The two are huddled so closely that they seem to be a single body. A flesh made one by the cold and the proximity of nightfall and a foreboding of death. Pastoseco shrugs his shoulders. He opens his eyes.

One way or the other, it's all the same, thinks the captain, and, without taking his eyes off the Indian, he slips the pair of wings out of his pocket. The Indian holds them in his fingertips, lifting them to his eyes. The two men are staring at each other this way, a few inches apart, one each side of the badge, when the Indian asks if he can have them.

'Hey, soldier, give them to me,' he says.

'Sir,' says Losa.

And the Indian seems to be trying to understand; in the end, he does and says, 'Give them to me, sir.'

'Are you going to learn to keep in step without the grass?' asks Losa.

'Of course, sir.'

'Take them, then,' says Losa.

Again the Indian lifts the badge to his star-speckled eyes, peers at the captain over the top of the wings – peers at him for a moment or so as if he is seeing him for the first time – looks away, and then, opening his mouth wide, begins to laugh in such a way that little by little Losa is infected and he too laughs,

[143]

and for a long while the two of them, there at the bottom of the abyss, are convulsed with laughter.

Ten minutes later, Captain Losa lights a match and looks at his watch. The time is up. In the darkness, Pastoseco is whistling the same tune as always.

'What's that you're always whistling?' asks the captain.

'I don't know. It's from a long time ago, from when there was nothing. The Indians whistled it in the reed beds.'

'Well, brother,' says the other man. 'There's no rescue party. Climb up.'

Pastoseco, on top of the captain, reaches the lip; losing his footing once or twice, the Indian catches hold of the edge and climbs out of the pit. The air is colder up here but more breathable than the air below. He scans the sky for the first stars and decides on his course. Mounting his mule, he sets off whistling. Before long he is a dot in the distance.

The silence of the night is now complete.

COUSINS

Santiago Sylvester

The only good thing about making a stopover in an unfamiliar city is that you feel no need to form an opinion about the place. When the plane had landed safely and taxied to a halt, the stewardess's voice came over welcoming us; we then trooped majestically under a canopy towards the terminal building, a slow march that could have taken place to the accompaniment of Gregorian chant or snatches of grand opera. Instead, we arrived to the twang of the native harp playing a well-known traditional air.

Our plane had not been full, so that disembarkation was quick. I helped the woman in the next seat with her enormous holdall and found myself loaded down with another even larger package, a satchelful of stones, a coffer of coins, or a shipment of gold bullion, with which the good lady was about to flout the regulations; neither her repeated smiles nor her apologies eased the effort I was making or the ache in my shoulder. The two hundred yards to the baggage hall could hardly have been called a stroll, especially with the smuggled goods belonging to the lady, whose only contribution was to trot along beside me brimming over with thanks. The pitiless sun left no doubts that we were born into this world to suffer. In addition to which, I was carrying as hand luggage a woollen overcoat that I hadn't been able to fit into my suitcase and that was going to be no use here.

An unpleasant surprise lay in store for me. My connection was scheduled not for that afternoon but for the following day. This was clear enough in the timetables I was shown, a sentence against which there was no appeal and for which the airline disclaimed responsibility. Despite my complaints, all I got from the woman at the desk was infuriating courtesy: 'I'm afraid your information is inaccurate, sir.' The smuggler lady

[147]

tried to console me, but by then I wasn't having any more of that; so, with my shoulder dislocated and a feeling of being thoroughly put upon, I faced the problem of having to change money and find a hotel for the night. Clearing customs was quick. Routine questions with precious little cordiality, which was exactly what I gave in return, but I was soon on my own, at a loss and defeated by the heat, in a large area that looked as if it had once been a Nissen hut. People milled about to kill time, not knowing what else to do – passengers guilty of having inaccurate information or perhaps seekers who had lost the faith – but I had no time just then to verify anything because a bus was waiting to take us into the city.

The highway was narrow and monotonously straight; the vegetation sprang from the very edge of the tarmac and quickly thickened, only occasionally opening up and allowing a glimpse of distant mountains. All at once there was a clearing, and we stopped in the middle of the road, it being assumed that nothing would come from either direction. Some men with chainsaws turned and waved to us. Our driver took a package from the front seat and, leaving the engine running, climbed down with no explanation and swaggered off self-importantly. He stopped and spoke at some length to a well-built man in an open shirt and straw hat, who gestured with his head, his arms hanging motionless by his sides. The two looked like friendly neighbours making a deal of some sort; then they said good-bye, the gang waved to us with a fair amount of bantering that we couldn't catch, and the driver returned with that swagger he was so proud of.

The road widened into a dual carriageway with palm trees down the centre, and in the distance were single-storey adobe houses whose corrugated-iron roofs flashed bright signals that neither the sun nor anyone seemed disposed to pay attention to. White smoke, or dust, rose from a derelict site, a charcoal oven, a lime pit, or a yard where adobe bricks were being cut, but we turned sharply right and entered the city proper, leaving the smoke to its own business.

We were set down at a spacious, shaded office block, where I would willingly have stayed until the next day. It was an oasis of air-conditioning and background music in the heart of a dusty, tumbledown, deserted city whose inhabitants, having formed an opinion about their home town, had evidently gone off elsewhere. Here the branch of a bank operated – its name too much for one small window – and I was able to change money and find out about two or three hotels that had a common lack of imagination: they were all equally expensive. This time I allowed the smuggler lady to help me, and she told me the way to a cheap guest-house. It was called the Baby Sheraton, but I did not let that scare me off.

I tried ringing Celia from the guest-house; no luck, international calls were only available at the Telephone Exchange. In no fit state to walk the six blocks there, I accepted the landlady's offer to dispatch someone round to the post office to send Celia a cable. She and I had promised ourselves a formal dinner with candles and that sparkling wine she is so fond of. My delay would be a disappointment, but she at least was spared having to set foot in the Baby Sheraton.

It was a big, rambling old house that had not long since received a timely lick of whitewash. That you could still smell paint might have led to the unfounded conclusion that the place was clean and respectable. It consisted basically of a large flagstoned courtyard so choked with plants that it was hard to breathe – palms, ferns, fleshy-leaved and perhaps carnivorous plants, swaying listlessly like a herd of elephants. Only a pair of tortoises dared venture into this jungle. A wide verandah ran round the courtyard on all four sides. In one corner stood 'the porter's lodge', a square table that was piled with receipts, letters, and old newspapers and that had a drawer which the landlady opened very gingerly. A telephone lent prestige to this clutter, and a pair of quite reasonable armchairs acted as a lobby. Above the verandah lay the bedrooms, with their louvred shutters that darkened the interiors while allowing air, snores, and the odd squabble to float through. I was allotted one of the first-floor rooms, which looked on to a makeshift terrace, where a bathroom with a washbasin had been built; it was

[149]

reached by an unroofed, concrete staircase whose only appeal
was its solidity. The room was large and the sheets clean;
the one condition I exacted was that they change the bar of
soap in the lavatory, a soft lump full of hairs, which the
cleaning woman took away in her fingertips as if it were a
lizard.

The tall iron bedstead went well with the wardrobe, a hulk-
ing great piece of furniture with a cracked mirror. A small
revolving fan that whirred to the limit of its capacity brought
some relief. Excessive heat only admits the present or blots it
out; it does not allow you to do much in the way of making plans
or recalling the past; it shelves everything else in the effort to
survive. Even so, I remembered that, if the wind had not blown
him elsewhere, Rafael Iríbar – whose name came to me together
with two or three anecdotes of our days at the university – lived
hereabouts. Deciding to look him up, I promptly fell asleep. A
deafening clap of thunder, an explosion in the wardrobe, woke
me, and I heard rain in the courtyard. An unexpected thunder-
storm; I hadn't seen the clouds gather. When I mentioned this
to the landlady, she said, 'It's always like that here' – a remark I
was to hear often in reference to almost everything.

I looked Rafael up in the telephone book, but he wasn't there.
The landlady told me that Silvia might be able to help me. 'She
knows everybody.' And she turned to a woman whom I noticed
for the first time. She was only a few feet away, in one of the
lobby armchairs, sitting with exaggerated formality, perhaps to
compensate for the hair rollers that deformed her head. Her
most apparent occupation was that of painting her nails; she
smiled to herself in a manner that did not suit her, accentuating
her nose and revealing too many teeth for one smile. 'Perhaps I
do,' she said. 'I shall have to speak to a girl friend who has
everybody's number. Rafael Iríbar, did you say?'

'Yes, Rafael Iríbar.'

And she went to her room to look for something.

A while later, there was a knock at my door. I was shaving, so
I opened it with lather all over my face. It was Silvia, her hair in
a middle parting and pinned back above the ears with matching

clasps. I apologized for my appearance, but she didn't mind. 'It makes me look not so bad,' she said, patting her hair in recollection of the rollers. The new hairstyle had improved her smile, and I told her so. She said I looked better too. It wasn't exactly a compliment, but I thanked her for the slip of paper she handed me with my friend's phone number.

It was dark by the time Rafael came to pick me up. He hadn't changed much, but no one would have taken him for a student now. A double-breasted blue suit and a rather self-important way of speaking distanced him from those somewhat tedious student afternoons that lacked all urgency and left him without a degree, which, it must be admitted, he had given little real evidence of ever seeking. He took a step back to look at me: 'You haven't changed a bit.'

A pointless observation. It's what people always start with before they're sure whether it is true or not. As we were both thinking this same thing, we made a show of friendliness and good manners and changed the subject.

The storm had left the night cool and starry; the courtyard jungle, as grateful as we were, gave off a scent strong enough to have laid out anyone of an excitable nature. By contrast, the street – which I had only seen once – was as depressing as before, lit by the swaying beam of an overhead spotlight. Rafael had brought his car; as we were about to drive off, Silvia came out with two women friends, all three of them dressed in white. They were so noisy it made them sound like a crocodile of schoolgirls in heat; as they passed us they made a number of cheeky cracks which told me that Rafael knew them. He made no comment.

From what I could make out, my guest-house was not in the centre; eight blocks off the main square put it outside the heavy traffic, a distance that in this town no one went on foot. At the corner, Silvia and her group were waiting for a bus. They turned round as we drove past, but by this time Rafael and I were exchanging biographical information in a conversation that had to cover a number of years to get down to the present.

All the same, I said: 'One of those girls got me your phone number.'

'Of course, it's ex-directory. Silvia?'

'Yes. She made some inquiries and tracked you down.'

He laughed in the dark, flattered.

We talked about friends neither of us had seen for years, and this enabled us once again to draw conclusions about the passage of time. He was married, had three children, and for the last six years had owned an ironmongery, a shop that ran itself. And so we reached the square, another jungle, whose virtue was that its trees had grown in pleasing confusion. We parked the car and went for a stroll; Rafael kept bumping into acquaintances. In the middle of the square stood an Italian fountain – or what passed for one – featuring impressively coloured jets of water, an object which was something of a tourist attraction thereabouts. Fruit-laden orange trees lined the paths; someone had vigorously realized an aesthetic principle by whitewashing all the stones. Surrounded by shaggy banana trees and palms that lent anonymity to several pairs of lovers, the rose garden lay in shadow. We went across to a bar; after an all-round exchange of pleasantries that didn't seem to lead anywhere, we moved on to another bigger bar, where we sat by a window that opened on to the square.

'Let's have a drink and then go home. Bettina's expecting us. She wants to meet you.' Then, out of the blue, he said: 'Inquiries, my foot. She phoned straight to me.'

I didn't know what he was talking about.

'Silvia, your friend from the hotel.'

'Ah, yes, my friend – the one whose name is all I know about her, except that she paints her nails on the verandah.'

'She called to say a friend of mine was looking for me. She didn't know your name. It was just an excuse to talk to me.'

It didn't seem a boast, and I couldn't think of anything to say. He added something trivial about the call, and that was all he confided.

He lived in a big house, set back in a well-tended garden. It was an elegant neighbourhood, quiet and full of trees. I made a light remark, invoking words of his from the past. One night he had come looking for me and had found me behind a stack of books, bleary-eyed and on the border of insanity over an approaching exam. 'What are you doing there!' he said. 'Isolated like the oligarchy!' I reminded him of this as we were going in, but he was quick to deflect the blow.

'Nothing of the kind,' he said. 'I'm a victim: God sentenced me to resign myself to the best.'

That was how he spoke, in well-turned, cynical phrases, saying the opposite of what he meant. It was in this more than anything else that I recognized my old friend.

Bettina was a slender girl whose fragility was accentuated by an ungainly mass of over-pale hair; her most flirtatious gesture was to toss it from one side of her head to the other, so that she seemed in a perpetual daze. She was holding dinner back for us. We crossed an octagonal entrance hall, with a black and white tiled floor, and went into a cosy little living-room, where a group of people was gathered. Rafael introduced me as an old friend, and then I noticed that, not wearing a jacket and tie, I was not dressed for the occasion. I made some sort of conventional joke about this that was received in the same spirit. Then we all went into the dining-room.

I was seated between María Jesús, Rafael's sister, and a pretty, cross-eyed girl, whose squint was yet another adornment, an added way of attracting attention, and who could do nothing but laugh politely the whole evening. A grandiose centrepiece of flowers and branches made it impossible to see across the table, but it enabled one to hold an intimate conversation. Otherwise, this long, elaborate table would have turned any conversation into a symposium. María Jesús devoted her whole attention to listening to me; she knew more about me, or so at least she hinted, than I did myself. Her husband, a thickset, hairy man, planted like a tree opposite us, also brought up anecdotes about me, doubtless invented by Rafael. I had once hoisted a shirt up the flagpole of a girl's school as a signal inviting the pupils to a party. That bit was true, but not the alleged consequence that the girls had turned up and that the police had had to come and take them away. Nor was there any truth in the alcoholic indiscretion that had me passing out fully clothed in someone else's bed because supposedly I'd said: 'I always sleep like this.' On the other hand, it was true that one night I had loaded a piano on to a lorry, intending to give a serenade.

'He seems very serious now,' María Jesús commented to her brother.

'A married man.'

'Married! Then away with you at once!' I have no idea what Rafael's sister thought I was going to get up to, but she seized on the example she had opposite her to infer that all men are cheats. 'The only thing marriage guarantees is that you'll cheat.'

'Why? It doesn't show in my face, does it?' it occurred to me to say.

'If that's the way you are, it will show up somewhere.'

At that, the conversation broke up into total confusion, and everyone shouted at once, suddenly excited, as at the sound of an unexpected doorbell. María Jesús waved her arms above the table, talking to right and left according to which way the conversation went; her hair, which was prematurely white, combined with her girlish face to produce a mystery that she used to good effect. Someone said something objectionable, and she turned to me, red-faced and angry: 'That's not very nice.'

'Not very nice,' I echoed without knowing what she was talking about. And so, speaking of things that had nothing to do with anyone – or that could have had to do with everyone – that deceptively formal dinner proceeded with the aid of a silent maid, who came and went like a ghost with food and drink.

Back in the living-room everyone calmed down. Mozart helped out with a sonata chosen by Rafael. The beautiful, cross-eyed girl emerged from her silence to ask, 'Is that Mozart's sonata?' And she retreated back into it, a bit rattled when Rafael replied, 'It was, but I don't know whose it is now.' The confusion returned; it was the group's style, their way of amusing themselves with fragments of talk that skipped from subject to subject. In different circumstances, this living-room would have promoted meditation, being large and rather gloomy, with heavy furniture – evidence perhaps of a substantial inheritance – and walls hung with portraits, tapestries, and ceramic plates. This carefully wrought harmony was broken only by a few Velázquez reproductions (a hundred pesetas at the Prado) which, to make matters worse, had been found worthy of carved-wood frames. Bettina sat down beside me. She was tired and flicked her blonde hair from side to side but she perked up like the good hostess she was brought up to be whenever someone asked her a question. 'Are you leaving tomorrow?'

'Yes, in the afternoon. Barring surprises.'

'What surprises?'

'That's exactly what surprises are, a surprise. What I mean is, assuming the plane shows up and I'm at the airport. Or the other way round.'

A while later, the scene had changed. We moved around according to a private arrangement that did not necessarily have anything to do with our interest in any given conversation. Mozart had yielded to Louis Armstrong, and he to the boleros of the Mexican singer Ortiz Tirado, but they too passed as unnoticed as a guardian angel. I had tucked myself away in a corner, propped against a piano; there María Jesús appeared with a bottle of cognac, which was welcome.

'You're leaving tomorrow?'

I had already answered that question once and I gave the same reply: 'In the afternoon, barring surprises.'

I wanted to explain that Celia was expecting me, and I was upset because I did not know whether my cable had reached her, but María Jesús cut me short: 'Never explain, my friend; all of us here are just passing through.' I lent an ear, and, just as she was about to confirm a suspicion of mine that something was going on here, Rafael came up and dragged me to the other end of the room, where they needed someone to settle an argument about fighting cocks. 'There's no point in coming to me for that one,' was all I could say, but I'd been removed from the danger zone.

The party came to an end when the first couple left; everyone found it was late by then, and in an instant the reason for our being there changed, as if it had crumbled away. Wide-awake but glum, Rafael tried to make us stay on a while, but he was not all that convincing. By now Bettina had ceased to hide her weariness and was just keeping her end up with the aid of a fixed smile and the hope of being in bed soon. María Jesús said good-bye with a 'See you soon' all round, and again it seemed to me that she had an ulterior motive when she asked me whether I'd made up my mind about leaving.

Rafael drove me back to my hotel, suggesting on the way that I stay for a couple of days: 'There are some parties on the horizon. We can go out to the country.' But the invitation was a bit forced, and I said good-bye without committing myself. Some men were sweeping the streets; all that was missing was a pack of cats running loose to convince us that the end of the world was at hand.

Two of the lodgers started fighting in the courtyard because, in revenge for something, one of them had turned on the radio while the other was still asleep. Having been wakened too early, I got up; a rule I'm forced to obey dictates that once awake I can't get back to sleep again. A quarter of an hour later, I had washed my face and combed my hair and, technically lucid, was having breakfast in the guest-house dining-room, a rectangular room with a plank floor that creaked and bounced up and down at each step. Silvia was there, hair on end and bleary-eyed; she smiled at me out of sheer habit, and I felt obliged to join her.

'Life doesn't work out very well in the morning,' I said by way of greeting.

'Not in the morning, no; but perhaps it did last night.'

I took this to mean she was testing the water. With her face unmade up she looked tired, but she knew how to make naturalness conquer unfavourable impressions. Another good point was her long, elegant hands, which she did not use excessively.

She wasn't pretty but, by making the best of herself, she had a certain appeal.

'It was quite an evening,' I said. 'And now I'm suffering for it. All my bones ache.' I thanked her again for helping me to contact Rafael, and immediately I saw that it was he she wanted to talk about.

'What's the monster have to say for himself?'

'He brought me home. He has some nice friends – '

' – and a charming wife.' She was obviously longing to bring this subject up too.

I had to tell her all about the party, who was there, what they talked about (had they talked about anything?), and above all whether Rafael had been brilliant, boring, amusing, or whatever; she drew the conclusions. She knew everyone there and, in one way or another, despised them all equally. 'María Jesús' head is full of ravings and silly pretensions. She's terribly frustrated; she wishes her husband was a distinguished man – you must have seen that for yourself. Bettina is a ridiculous prude. She has given Rafael three children without ever letting him see her naked.'

'How would you know?' This conversation was getting on my nerves.

'I know.' It was a dry, definitive reply. But it was eleven o'clock by then, and I had to be off to Aerolíneas to confirm my flight.

My guest-house, in a quiet street with a warehouse on every corner, was right off the beaten track. But towards the centre the streets grew more and more crowded until, on the far side of an avenue that served as a dividing line, the pavements narrowed, crammed shop windows displayed radios cheek by jowl with bedroom slippers, and there was bustle everywhere you looked. Certain shops, partial to noisy publicity, advertised special offers over loudspeakers. I came across my smuggler friend, transformed into a venerable lady; she was in a little white hat which quite suited her. We greeted each other like old acquaintances, exchanged deeply felt opinions on planes and forced stopovers, and we said good-bye, happy to have met up

again. As I got to Aerolíneas, I passed a young man pushing a baby in a pram; smiling too much, he looked ill at ease; perhaps, without wishing to, he was making an ideological point. The annoyingly polite young woman attended me: 'Your plane leaves at seven. If you're taking the bus, you must be here two hours earlier. Thank you.' An impeccable smile was the sign that she had finished with me.

The square was quite different in daylight; the trees had a new stateliness, but the flower beds seemed less tidy, and the paths were littered and dirty. Night selects what it shows, while the day reveals all, presenting things in both their splendour and decay. Night is timeless, while the day cannot escape the passing of time. I sat in a café with a view of the square; preoccupied men kept coming in, looking round, and leaving again without finding what they were after. At a nearby table two men were talking business with the sort of words, gestures, and aggressive strategy that I had rid my life of. The waiter brought me a beer, and I turned my attention to it with that feeling of contentment expressed in the old saying, 'Live and let live.'

At the guest-house two messages awaited me. One from Silvia: 'I'd like to speak to you.' The other said: 'Señorita María Jesús rang. She is expecting you at seven this evening at La Alcancía, a teashop on the corner of the square next to the Astor Cinema.' From one of the rooms came a lively song, perhaps over the radio which had been the bone of contention; above the courtyard glided two pigeons, only to land heavily on the gutter. With the messages in my hand, I must have been the picture of confusion, because the landlady asked: 'Bad news?'

'No.'

'Good, then?' I didn't know what to answer, but she continued her prodding. 'You're staying on, are you?' A piece of presumption. Was she, as I was, impatient for the outcome? 'I have to know so as to reserve the room.'

'I'm not sure yet. I'll let you know.'

The second message, of course, was the one that bothered me. It would have been a lot easier had María Jesús talked to

me; her tone of voice, an explanatory word would have helped. But this way, without anything to go on, her words were altogether too neutral. I left the messages on the bedside table. The wardrobe's cracked mirror carried a worrying symbolism. All I needed was a hat to be the character in a private-eye film who is always smoking in tatty hotels – a hat and a woman marching up and down in a petticoat. I made up my mind to trust in fate (which is never done in private-eye films): if I could change my flight to the following day I could meet her. As for Silvia, I found her in her room and invited her to lunch.

I phoned Aerolíneas and once more I discovered that it is not only fate that provides solutions: 'There is no flight tomorrow; you can't leave until the day after.' It seemed reasonable enough; suspense makes its own rules, and I had to accept them. 'It's all right,' I was told. 'We've cancelled your flight, but you must come by the office before five o'clock. Thank you.' Again the thank you, a professional oversight, since neither of us had anything to thank the other for.

Silvia looked wonderful; a floral sundress left her shoulders bare, and she moved with great expertise on high-heeled white sandals. We went to a nearby restaurant with a cheerful look about it. Inevitably, it had to be cheap; four corner tables, a waiter who stood there doing nothing, a steamy atmosphere redolent of regional food.

'Thanks for the invitation.' She was wearing her hair loose, and this gave movement and energy to her head. 'You must have thought my message somewhat forward, but I had to talk to you. When are you leaving?'

'I keep being asked that. Either everyone wants me to leave or there is a general lack of imagination.'

'In my case it's neither; I don't want you to leave, not yet, nor do I lack imagination. On the contrary, my imagination's operating under full steam.' She then moved her long, elegant hand to open the menu.

There was not much choice; I ordered a casserole of peas, and Silvia roast beef and potatoes. The waiter made a mental note of our order, his expression indicating that his mind was elsewhere, and as he went off he whisked the dust from the other tables. Silvia and I sized each other up across the table; then, without more ado, she drew a packet of letters out of her bag and gave me one to read: 'They're from Rafael.'

I didn't like it; I saw something underhand about her asking me to pry into my friend's life. Noting my hesitation, she took the letter out of its envelope herself: 'Don't worry, the prose is good.' With that, I gave in. It began: 'My darling Titch –'

'Titch?'

'That's me,' she said, her face expressionless. 'That's what he calls me.'

I didn't laugh. 'While you read this, I will, as ever, be thinking of you. I have no idea when I'll be able to hold you in my arms again, but just thinking about your hair and mouth and breasts, which ring truer than the cathedral bell, makes my blood boil and the sleeping partner between my legs begin to stir.' This, I thought, was far enough. I looked at her as if to say what's it to do with me, and I gave the letter back.

'They're all from him.' So what? I wanted to say. 'Look at the date of that one.' It was dated a few months earlier.

'I wasn't exactly of the opinion that they were your childhood pen-pal letters.' I could not see what she was after. I said that anyone who kept letters was only laying up a store of future gossip, hoping that somebody else (in this case me) would eventually read them. She laughed in spite of herself, then, turning to the waiter, snarled: 'Antonio, what's happened to the food? Have they gone to slaughter the cow?' She looked at me with studied politeness; she had grown quite pretty, perhaps in an erotic reaction to the good prose.

'You must understand, the reason I showed you that letter was not because I'm an exhibitionist. I need you to do me a favour. For reasons that are beside the point, I haven't been able to see Rafael recently.'

'It's probably because Bettina –'

'– is a stupid woman who bores him silly. Would you believe it if I told you he's in love with me, not Bettina?'

'Fine, I believe you.' I was not at all sure about it.

Antonio appeared with the food, and this gave us a respite. Again we sized each other up like two boxers. The food was good, of the unclassifiable kind dubbed home cooking. The house wine, in keeping with the restaurant's prices, was a bit on the tart side.

'A girl friend of mine is giving a party tomorrow. I want you to come and bring him.'

'You want to use me.'

She gave an irritated wave of the hand: 'A man with morals. What a come-down!'

'I'm no moralist, but if I am asked to do something I want to know what my part is. Not to mince words, I'm to be a go-between.'

'I thought you'd been away in a civilized country, but I see they are as wishy-washy there as the rest of us.'

'Marvellous! You want me to pimp so as to save national honour.'

She chuckled to herself; I was outplayed. 'All right, I want to use you; but I promise to be on the level. Incidentally, I'll introduce you to a friend who wants to meet you.'

'The old, old game, is it?'

'Yes.'

'No, thanks. I've a date today, and whether or not I can make your party depends on how that works out.'

'A heavy date, I'm sure.' She knew how to score a bull's-eye.

'Tell me something: why don't you just phone him – like yesterday?'

'I know my own business. You shouldn't ask me to tell you my life history just because you're doing me a favour.' She stared down at her plate; when she raised her head she was no longer so full of herself, and her voice sounded dejected, unsure. 'I don't know if he will want to see me again. I have my pride too.'

Perhaps she was being theatrical, but these things always get to me; as the tango lyric says, she got in under my guard, and I promised to give Rafael her message. The wine was acrid, but I raised my glass to propose a toast: 'That's the way it is here, right?'

'That's the way it is everywhere,' and she smiled.

My meeting with María Jesús was not so interesting. I arrived at La Alcancía on the dot of seven, but she wasn't there. A sixth sense urging me to be discreet, I opted for a neutral zone and sat down at a table at the back. The place was on the pretentious side, chandeliers with crystal prisms, net curtains, turned-wood furniture. An illuminated sign offered *Güisqui*, which I had to read twice before I worked out what it meant. It doesn't surprise me that the word has been accepted by the Spanish Royal Academy; one day they'll accept *Jóligud*, a faraway land, reputed to have been a real place, where the bioscope turned into the cinema.

My first surprise was to find that everyone there knew María Jesús. Hardly my idea of a secret assignation! My second was that she felt I had chosen a rather gloomy spot, and she whisked me off to a table by the window, centre stage. That put us in the limelight – all we needed now was the applause. She had on a black suit of the kind worn by a lay order and also, as it happened, a pair of secular earrings. At the same time, her eyes were made up to such an extent that they almost warned you to be on the lookout. The contradiction in her appearance was guaranteed to make any man interested.

'I'm glad you didn't catch that plane,' she said as if we had just met by chance. My reply was to pull her message out of my pocket and hand it to her. 'What a funny description,' she remarked. '"A teashop on the corner of the square next to the Astor Cinema." All you needed was a map to stop you getting lost.'

'I wanted to see you; I'd have made it even without directions.'

She looked out of the window, greeted two or three passers-by, made a witty remark to someone at the next table, and finally called the waiter and ordered a cocktail. I asked for a whisky; had they brought me a *güisqui* I would have sent it back. When I drink something I want to know what it is. I felt an itching at the back of my neck, a warning that I was running low on patience.

'I phoned you for Rafael. He's been out all day and couldn't call you himself; he wants to have a little get-together tonight in your honour.' And with an unconvincing change of emphasis she added that they had all been delighted with me. This was not what I was hoping for.

I know I'm reckless, even inexperienced; in point of fact, experience comes only when you have made so many mistakes that the very word sounds ridiculous. I made a pass at her, reaching for her hand. 'I put off leaving because of your message, not because of Rafael.' She didn't withdraw it but she became so uncomfortable that I ended up taking my own away. It was a good thing there was background music; her silence would have been a scream of reproach. I was in no mood to apologize; anyway, I hoped she would. And so there we were, stuck in a disjointed conversation that neither of us knew how to end, until Bettina and Rafael arrived. Just when I should have been winging my way above the earth, I had to adjust my behaviour to receive the spellbinding homage of my friends.

This consisted of traipsing from one place to another. They enjoyed the job of showing me round the city. They took me to a park with a privet hedge which had a botanical garden, a lake with ducks, a donkey for tourists to be photographed on, a temporarily closed dance floor, and an air-conditioned café, where we had a beer. Then we went down an avenue of *ceibos* and *lapachos* that led to a river; we threw pebbles in the water and looked for shooting stars in the sky. The spectacle of fireflies, a hail of sparks beyond the scope of our humdrum exclamations of praise, lifted me out of my bad mood. At that point, in another attempt to make overtures to María Jesús, I laid my hand as if by accident on her hip, and she, in the same way, removed it. Bettina, a denser patch of darkness within the darkness, said happily: 'You seem to have met with a surprise, then?'

'Yes, my plane came in, but I wasn't at the airport.' I don't know if there is anything more disconcerting than innocence.

On our return to the city, I sat in the back seat beside María Jesús, but I kept an angry distance. The radio was blaring rhythmically, and Rafael only turned it down to point out an indistinct clump of trees: 'That field should have been mine. It belonged to my grandfather. That is why the world's going the way it is: farmers are now business men and vice versa.' He caught my eye in the rearview mirror. 'I'm the product of my father's bad business sense.' And he threw his head back in a laugh. Up went the volume again, isolating us each in our own thoughts and making it look as though Rafael didn't want to talk. Bettina jabbered away with María Jesús, and even though they were shouting it was impossible to hear what they said. At one point they laughed, and María Jesús fell against me, only to spring back as if she had touched a live wire. I looked at her out of the corner of my eye; she had suddenly become serious, on her guard. I was glad; at least it showed that she didn't trust me. The game of treacherous cat and wretched mouse had been humiliating.

We stopped at a noisy place, too dark for us to see what was going on. I was hungry, but they said we'd be meeting up with María Jesús' husband later for dinner. So any notion I entertained of physical fraternizing was out the window for good. For good? We shouldn't say things like for good or limit our options with words like now or never, which dramatize our lives and are usually not true. So I went on hoping anyway, while pretending to myself that I wasn't. Bettina dragged me off for a dance. Though I've always been a rotten dancer (always? here we go again!), even I could tell that she moved as if she were completely at home. She told me she hadn't danced for ages, but it didn't seem like it. I suppose that dancing is like swimming or good manners; once you've learnt them you don't forget them. 'I never dance nowadays. You don't know your friend Rafael. He's not very sociable.' She was like a little girl who had just been rewarded with an ice cream. I was feeling almost tender towards her, which was why I decided to apply an outrageous piece of logic which, for some obscure reason beyond my control, I found stimulating. If I was going to keep my word to Silvia, it would have to be then, while Bettina was feeling more comfortable with me. It was the logic of the scoundrel, who would rather be an out-and-out bastard than a pale imitation. I took Rafael aside and told him we were invited to a party. His reaction, straight out of the best school of poker, was aloof: 'We'll see.' He did not go into confidences or involve me unnecessarily. I was grateful for this, but when he went back to the table his manner seemed more reserved.

We stayed until it was time to meet María Jesús' husband. They took me to their club, which was nearby – a big house with double doors that lay open on to a lighted drawing-room. The dining-room was another salon with one or two gracious touches. Mirrors, curtains, and the odd dollop of formality lent the place an air of elegance. We chose a large table – 'in case anyone else turns up' – beside a wood stove, luckily just a decoration. Suspended from the ceiling at intervals were slowly revolving fans which made the plants in the shadowy corners keep bowing. María Jesús had begun a low-key flirtation with me, an unfair ploy based on safety – the imminent arrival of her loving spouse. This was an unutterable bore. I am prepared to put up with being made to work, or even with being shown I'm wrong, but not with being bored. This goes for people, books, plays, and scholarly footnotes, and I think of myself as intolerant. So I began to talk to Bettina and Rafael, giving María Jesús to understand that I was leaving her out. She sat quietly until her husband arrived. He seemed to have just come from a football match, military manoeuvres, or a procession of penitents. His belly stuck out of an open shirt, his tie was loose, his face was purple, and his hair stood on end. We all stared in suspense. María Jesús went rigid, Rafael cracked a joke ('looks like your horse dumped you in it') and the husband gaped at us as if he couldn't understand what we were going on about.

'A disastrous day.' He made a half-hearted attempt to tidy his clothes. 'Disastrous.'

*

Reading newspapers has all the characteristics of a vice; it is inescapable and it solves none of our problems apart from its own necessity. War in the Lebanon. The arms race. A political volcano in Central America. Andreotti comes out with a truth that only an heir of Macchiavelli in cahoots with the Vatican could know ('Of course power corrupts, but mostly it corrupts those who don't have it'), when just then a waft of Chanel No 5 found me with my guard down and almost knocked me out: Silvia was coming in to breakfast. Wearing too much make-up for the time of day, she carried a leather handbag slung from her shoulder and wore a pair of butterfly-shaped dark glasses which seemed less for the sun than for enticement. A fit of nerves made her make more noise than necessary; she drew up a chair, plunked her bag on the table, took out a cigarette, asked the maid to hurry – 'I've got to fly' – and she only calmed down a little when I told her that her message had reached its destination.

'What did he say? I want the exact words.'

'He said, "We'll see."'

'That's not much. It means he'll come. And you?'

'I don't know, I may come too.'

'And that date of yours . . .' The fox, she remembered.

'It went well. But I keep my doors open.'

She drank her coffee in a gulp, barely touched her toast, lit a cigarette, and scampered off before she had finished it. 'See you tonight. Andrea will like you.' All that remained of her was a heady scent as I went back to my paper.

At midday I phoned Rafael; he wasn't there. Bettina told me he'd got out on the wrong side of the bed that morning, and after a fight provoked – so she said – by him, had stormed off without a word. Anger robbing her of any talent she had for economy, she filled in a host of details. Rafael had refused to put on some shirt or other, he had not taken the children to school, nor had he wanted to answer a phone call from his bank. I deduced, because it is not hard to put two and two together, that Silvia was right: Rafael would be at the party. In reply, I could only give Bettina a few clichés about passing storms, dog days, and the need to be understanding. But she went off on an unexpected tack: 'Don't you believe it; Rafael's crazy. Crazy or else a son of a bitch.' It was an explosion of words that had got into the wrong mouth. 'He picks a fight over the least little thing; he's frantic. I'd just as soon he made up his mind right now and cleared off altogether. He must have mentioned something to you. Are you free at all this afternoon?' It was the last thing I wanted. I'm hopeless in these situations, but people are always trying to confide in me. I attempted to pacify her, with dubious success, and I said good-bye.

I spent the afternoon in the guest-house, reading. After dozing for a while, I woke with a start. The heat was suffocating, and I flung open the window. Another storm was brewing. A flock of birds flew by looking for shelter, a gust of wind shook the plants as if hoping for some reaction from them, and the first drops fell, fat and noisy. A moment later it began to pour. Perhaps Bettina would be reminded of my remark, 'Every cloud has its silver lining.' But I didn't want to think about that; I'm not a purveyor of solutions. From my bed I heard the drone of the rain and the thunder rumbling overhead, and I smelled the rank smell of the earth as if all at once it had got up and moved. My courage extended to staying put and thinking of nothing at all until the storm had passed. By then night had fallen; I had a bath and left for the party.

Rafael hadn't arrived yet but Silvia had, and, laying it on thick – know-how, perfumes, scenic presence – she was impressive. Andrea, a redhead, who was the owner of the house, had a walk like certain boxers, short steps, body balanced, but she wasn't bad. I was introduced with the sort of flattering remark used to boost the image of someone just passing through whom no one knows anything about. It was a good start. Glass in one hand, a plate of cold food in the other, I was raring to go.

It was easy to see what this group of middle-aged city gents, smiling for no apparent reason, was after that evening. They wallowed with the solemnity of Spanish galleons on the seabed yet managed to give the impression of shiftiness. Maybe they were shifty. One of them made me regret that we don't practise the wise Japanese custom of greeting one another with little bows. I was drenched with a clinging scent and had to go to the bathroom to wash my hand.

In an armchair, one couple was engaged in living out a private squabble. She, a coarse-ish but by no means ugly platinum blonde, had decided with a vengeance to show off her legs. Her companion looked like a casino manager; his oiled hair was parted in the middle, and he wore an embroidered white waistcoat one could not but admire. Perhaps they were expecting a photographer.

Andrea told everyone to help themselves. A table laden with a whole selection of the things man has invented to ruin his liver offered food and drink, with a preponderance of salads. Some of the women, however, carried on as if they were the hostess and went around waiting on us hand and foot. Such admirable good will. Most of us were standing, which conferred mobility on the party. First I talked to a girl who wanted to see the world but who soon dropped me for a more obviously local interest. I moved on to a group engrossed in urban politics and this time it was I who abandoned them. From there I skipped to the disruptive laughter of a woman who seemed to have decided to finish off the party's whole supply of booze. An amiable man, whom I was about to ask if he hadn't come to the wrong door, drew my attention to some unusual word derivations. Eventually I approached a circle of men who were hiding their paunches and telling the girls risqué stories to make them laugh. When they found out that I was a bit of a globe-trotter, economy-class but nonetheless international, they changed the subject and talked about their own trips. Travel is a better conversational gambit than blue jokes; add to it total recall, and the way a traveller talks about his travels is the way a cook talks about meals. At least these men had the ability to express themselves that comes of the desire to look good.

As I was on my way to the drinks table, a man burst in from the street with all the gusto of someone distributing sweets to children. 'Ladies! Mad, wonderful ladies! Gather round!' A bit of an old reprobate, in spite of himself he brought colour to the party. A well-cut grey suit and blue tie with matching hand-kerchief in his breast pocket made him look as though he were about to launch into heroic tales of the stock market. But he had other plans. 'I'm after beautiful womanhood; ugly ones needn't step forward.' You had to admire his sales technique. He was generally gracious and had an appropriate word to say to each and every one of them, from which I saw he was something of a fixture on the local night scene. A number of women immediately flocked to him, Silvia greeted him briefly and introduced me, and then the man made a trial circuit before grounding in exactly the right spot – between two women ostensibly fighting over him, each pledged to glorify mankind's legendary link with the forbidden fruit.

When Rafael arrived, I was having a crack at the tango. I nodded to him, incorporating this into my step, and went on dancing. Most of the men, having been bred to do just that, had advanced on the women, who, in their turn, did nothing to protect themselves. My sporadic conversations with Andrea had been encouraging, but you can never tell until the end; recent experiences counselled me not to delude myself. Then, because that's the way life is, I found myself on my own, watching the party from a distance. To be truthful, I didn't know what to do with myself, so, in search of my destiny and a chair, I went into a little room nearby, and there were Silvia and Rafael. They didn't notice me, so I crept away to another room.

Andrea saw me come in; she was besieged by a tall man with a chubby face that made him look like a spoiled child. She signalled to me to go to her. 'This fellow's barmy,' she said when I reached her.

'And I love you,' I said into her ear.

'I don't.' She seemed to think that witty, because she laughed theatrically.

The spoiled brat took her by the arm. 'You've already abandoned me once; twice would be intolerable. I shall kill myself.' He had something of the cheerful lush about him – he was certainly both of those.

'You might not believe it, my love, but you'll learn to live without me.'

'Yes, like the donkey in the story: just when he learned to live without eating he died.'

Andrea lifted her red hair with her hands and let it fall. She suddenly seemed to cotton on and looked at him in pique. 'I'm no one's meal!' And the brat plumped for the all-purpose reply of laughter.

'We're all somebody's meal,' he said, but just then another man came up on the same errand as all the others, so that now we were a crowd. I suggested a tour of the house to Andrea, but guessing at my only-too-apparent motive, with which she obviously disagreed, she refused: 'I already know the house, thank you.' I slunk off to the drinks table alone.

It was no longer the moment for dancing, or we were simply enjoying a peaceful lull. The music had been turned down low, and this trumpet solo now playing was more in keeping with my mood. There was so much of everything that choosing a drink wasn't easy. Silvia came to my aid, but it made no difference. We opted for an *eau de vie* that kicked like a mule. Her recent conversation showing on her face, she couldn't stop smiling. She guessed what I was thinking, and for the first and last time I saw her blush.

Rafael had left. 'This party will go on for some time, and he has to get up early. He sends his regards.' It seemed to me that he could well have given me them himself, but I accepted the fact that he wanted to slip out unobserved. He had certainly succeeded in doing so. He had departed like a ghost who, instead of dragging his chains, prefers to vanish without trace.

'Rather beyond the call of discretion, wasn't it?' My words sounded like a reproach. Silvia looked at me as if to say let's be grown-ups. She was always right when it came to secrets.

Feeling generally predisposed towards the sedentary life, I had the luck to find an empty chair. We sat down at the far end of the long dining-room, which was connected to the adjoining room by an archway. A strategically placed mirror revealed that everything going on there was more or less the same as was

Cousins

going on here: euphoric conversations and couples who had embarked on a determined habeas corpus.

'You seem to have resolved your differences with Rafael.'

By way of reply she chose a mysterious look. 'And how are you making out with Andrea?'

'You can see for yourself; up to now, nothing doing. Neutral.'

'Don't be silly. Go after her, you've scored a hit. I'm letting you in on this hot tip for both your sakes.' I liked her cheekiness. 'I've done my bit.'

We chatted on in this way, openly plotting, until the elegant reprobate, who had by now made his choice, came up to us. What had finally convinced him was a curvaceous pair of hips.

'I'm celebrating my farewell to bachelorhood,' he said, and the woman clung to him, sweet as pie, confirming that she was a prize.

Silvia entered into the spirit of the game: 'Here's to the happy couple! And remember, I don't charge for being godmother.'

'You've got it wrong. I'm saying good-bye to my wild bachelor days in order to settle at last into confirmed bachelorhood.' And off they went, pleased with the joke, which, old though it was, nonetheless endorsed the agreement they had evidently come to.

Silvia's Chanel No 5 clung to my nostrils; I told her so, and she handed me a glass of whisky: 'The antidote.'

'If it's an antidote, I don't want it.' I handed it back; she stared at me with that smile of complicity. Suddenly she looked at her watch: 'I'm off right now! It's very late!' Picking up her handbag, she said in my ear: 'I'm leaving you with Andrea.'

'Yesterday you accused me of being a moralist, and I'm not sure I like that. I'm not, you know – '

'That's true, I apologize.'

' – which is why I want something else in payment. It's not your friend I want to go off with tonight but you.'

She was taken aback, then began to laugh so long and hard that she had to sit down. She took out a handkerchief to dry her eyes. Her make-up had begun to run – an attractive imperfection. Everything was working in her favour now; her thighs, bared in her tossing about, gave me a hint of her completely bare. When she could speak again, her voice was still not quite under control: 'That seems fair enough.'

Once out in the street, she said: 'I have to tell you, I fancy you. If I didn't, it wouldn't be worth the price.'

'I know. It was obvious all along we'd end up like this. We're so alike we could even be cousins.'

She hung on to my arm, offended: 'The nerve!'

At the guest-house we went to my room. I caught sight of myself again in the cracked mirror, a character out of a gangster film. I had a woman waiting for me now; all I needed was the hat.

I have always been amazed by the energy of those women who can go to bed at four in the morning, make love till six, stop only because the other party's worn out, and three hours later get up hungry. My explanation is that they don't drink alcohol; they are wise in a different way about the use of immoderation. The fact is that when she got up to leave I barely managed to open one eye and to ask her to wake me at one.

I wasn't wakened at one o'clock but at two, and it wasn't by her but by the landlady. There was a woman downstairs asking for me. I cursed the world but had to get a move on; I had three hours in which to shower, pack my case, eat something, and catch the bus.

It was Bettina. I must have looked awful, but she was in no state to notice such details. She was a pitiful sight, drawn and wearing dark glasses that blotted out a sleepless night. Rafael had walked out; this news brought me wide-awake. It wasn't the first time, she explained, but it might well be the last. 'He'd already made up his mind. It wasn't because of a quarrel, like the other times; he had it all worked out.' Knowing Rafael and I had been together the night before, which was only partly true, she wanted me to give her some clue, some fact that might help her. I swore I didn't know a thing. What else could I do? But I had a hunch and I told her to wait for me.

I found the landlady in the dining-room and asked if Silvia was there. 'She's checked out, sir, but she left you an envelope.' We went to the table in the courtyard, the porter's lodge, and the landlady handed me a sealed envelope. In it was a farewell message that brought our relationship to a coherent end: 'My undying love. I'll never forget you as long as I live.' And she signed it: 'Your carnal cousin,' underlining the second word. Were it not for the never-ending perversity of the world, this babble would have raised my spirits for days.

I couldn't calm Bettina down. Of course, I did not tell her what I knew, what I'd so easily guessed. I could only go on repeating like an idiot that Rafael would come back, as he invariably had, and I added something I always say, which I am proud of because it's my own invention: 'The history of a couple is the history of the pacts they make with each other.' It has the advantage of fitting anyone.

Notes on Contributors

MARCOS AGUINIS, born in Córdoba in 1935, graduated in medicine from the University of Buenos Aires and trained as a neurosurgeon in Paris, Cologne, and Freiburg. He now practises psychoanalysis in Buenos Aires. His novels are: *Refugiados: Crónica de un palestino* (1969); *La cruz invertida* (1970), which won the Planeta Prize; *Cantata de los diablos* (1972); *La conspiración de los idiotas* (1979); and *Profanación del amor* (1982). His books of stories, *Operativo siesta* (1978) and *Importancia por contacto* (1983), were reissued, with two later stories, as *Y la rama llena de frutos* (1986). The story printed here was written for this collection. Other works include *Maimónides, un sabio de avanzada* (1963), a biography; *El combate perpetuo* (1981), a fictionalized life of Guillermo Brown, the Irish-born Argentine admiral; *Carta esperanzada a un general* (1983), a polemic on the military mind; *El valor de escribir* (1985), essays on literature, psychoanalysis, Jewish themes, authoritarianism, and the problems of Argentine democracy; and *Un país de novela* (1988), a study of the Argentine character. He has been Secretary of Culture and currently, as an adviser to President Alfonsín, runs a programme for the democratization of Argentine culture.

JORGE ASÍS, born in 1946 in Avellaneda, an industrial suburb of Buenos Aires, has worked as a journalist on the Buenos Aires daily *Clarín*. His first book was poetry, *Señorita vida* (1970); then came *De cómo los comunistas se comen a los niños* (1971), humorous sketches, and *La manifestación* (1971), stories. Asís's other short fiction is published in *Fe de ratas* (1976), from which the story in this book is taken, and *La lección del maestro* (1987). He is also the author of eleven novels: *Don*

Abdel Zalim, el burlador de Domínico (1972); *La familia tipo* (1974); *Los reventados* (1974); the tetralogy *Flores robadas en los jardines de Quilmes* (1980), *Carne picada* (1981), *La calle de los caballos muertos* (1982), and *Canguros* (1983); *Diario de la Argentina* (1984); *Rescate en Managua/El pretexto de París* (1985); and *Partes de inteligencia* (1987). His articles have been collected in two volumes: *El Buenos Aires de Oberdán Rocamora* (1981) and *La ficción política* (1985). Asís, known as 'El Turco', comes of a Syrian family who emigrated from the Lebanon after the collapse of the Ottoman Empire. He is married, has four children, and has recently been an adviser to Carlos Menem, the Peronist candidate for the Argentine presidency.

ADOLFO BIOY-CASARES began writing as a boy, and by the age of twenty-three had published six books. He then wiped the slate clean and began all over again, in 1940, with the novel *La invención de Morel*, which won a Municipal Prize. Five others followed: *Plan de evasión* (1945), *El sueño de los héroes* (1954), *Diario de la guerra del cerdo* (1969), *Dormir al sol* (1973), and *La aventura de un fotógrafo en La Plata* (1985). His short fiction has been collected in: *La trama celeste* (1948); *Historia prodigiosa* (1956); *Guirnalda con amores* (1959); *El lado de la sombra* (1962), which won the Second National Prize; *El gran Serafín* (1967), which won the First National Prize; *El héroe de las mujeres* (1978); and *Historias desaforadas* (1986), from which the story in this book is taken. Other works are: *La otra aventura* (1969), essays and reviews; *Memoria sobre la pampa y los gauchos* (1970), on gaucho life; and *Breve diccionario del argentino exquisito* (1971), a compilation of Argentine commonplaces. With his wife Silvina Ocampo he wrote the detective novel *Los que aman, odian* (1962); with Jorge Luis Borges he created the first Argentine detective in *Seis problemas para don Isidro Parodi* (1942). Another of their inventions was the outrageous critic H. Bustos Domecq, whose activities are satirized in *Crónicas de Bustos Domecq* (1967) and

Nuevos cuentos de Bustos Domecq (1977). With Borges, he also founded a literary magazine, *Destiempo*, edited a series of detective fiction, compiled anthologies of poetry, short stories, gauchesco poetry, etc. His work has been called 'a parable that seems governed by the ideal of austerity'. The following have appeared in English: *The Invention of Morel and Other Stories* (1964), *Diary of the War of the Pig* (1969), *A Plan for Escape* (1975), *Chronicles of Bustos Domecq* (1976), *Asleep in the Sun* (1978), *Six Problems for don Isidro Parodi* (1981), and *The Dream of Heroes* (1987). He was born in Buenos Aires in 1914 and gave up the study of law to devote himself to writing.

ISIDORO BLAISTEN has worked in advertising, both as a photographer and writer; in journalism; and as a bookseller. Now a full-time author, he also holds writing workshops. His first book, *Sucedió en la lluvia* (1965) was poetry, which he still writes but does not publish. To date, the following story collections have appeared: *La felicidad* (1969), *La salvación* (1972), *El mago* (1974), *Cerrado por melancolía* (1982), and *Carroza y reina* (1986), from which his story here is taken. *Dublín al sur* (1980) and *A mí nunca me dejaban hablar* (1985) are selections from the above, and *Cuentos anteriores* (1982) is an omnibus volume. He is also the author of a volume of essays and reviews, *Anticonferencias* (1983). An unpublished novel, *Espérame mucho*, was the origin of a prize-winning film in 1983. Among other awards, Blaisten received a Municipal Prize in 1974, the Third National Prize for fiction in 1983, and the Second National Prize for essay and criticism in 1986. Born in Concordia, Entre Ríos, in 1933, Blaisten has lived in Buenos Aires for many years.

ANGEL BONOMINI, poet and short-story writer, was born in Buenos Aires in 1929. A small collection of later poetry, written between 1970 and 1980, has appeared under the title *Torres para el silencio* (1982). He worked as a journalist in New York for six years and has also been art critic for the Buenos Aires magazine *Panorama* and later for the newspaper *La Nación*. His short stories have appeared in four collections: *Los novicios de Lerna* (1972), which won a Second Municipal Prize; *Libro de los casos* (1975); *Los lentos elefantes de Milán* (1978); *Cuentos de amor* (1982); and *Historias secretas* (1985), from which the story in this book comes. *El mar* (1974), poems, and *Zodíaco* (1983), prose pieces, appeared with artwork by his wife, the painter Vechy Logioio. In 1971, he received a Fulbright grant.

ABELARDO CASTILLO was born in 1935, in San Pedro, in the Province of Buenos Aires. A playwright and story-writer, he founded two literary magazines, the polemical *El grillo de papel* (The Paper Cricket), in 1959, and *El escarabajo de oro* (The Gold Bug), in 1961; the former was closed by the police after six issues. He currently publishes a third, *El ornitorrinco* (The Duck-billed Platypus). His books of stories are: *Las otras puertas* (1961) and *Cuentos crueles* (1966), reprinted with additional tales as *Los mundos reales* (1972); *Las panteras y el templo* (1976); and *El cruce del Aqueronte* (1982). This last, from which the story here is taken, is a selection of older work both published and unpublished. *La casa de ceniza*, a novella, appeared in 1968. *El que tiene sed* (1985), a novel, obtained a First Municipal Prize. 'For Services Rendered' was written in response to the fatuous celebrations in 1979–80 of the Argentine army on the centenary of its extermination of the Indians in the campaign known to history as 'The Conquest of the Desert'. Castillo's plays include *El otro Judas* (1961), *Israfel* (1964), and *Sobre las piedras de Jericó* (1968). He also lectures and teaches a writing workshop. He is married to the author Sylvia Iparraguirre.

ESTELA DOS SANTOS, born in Buenos Aires in 1940, is the author of three volumes of stories, *Gutural y otros sonidos* (1965), *Las despedidas* (1972), and *Sanata triste* (1984).

[178]

Other works are: *El cine nacional* (1972), on Argentine films; *Las mujeres del tango* (1972) and *Las cantantes* (1979), on women tango singers; and *Las mujeres peronistas* (1983), a study of the effect on Argentine political life of woman suffrage, which was attained only in 1947. The story here is from her third book, which is redolent of the tango and is set in the 'thirties and 'forties in the less glamorous suburbs of Buenos Aires. A feminist, she says, 'My writing takes no ideological stance, it stems from an unprogrammed innermost self, which is why I can write stories about the world of the tango in spite of the fact that the tango is so male-dominated.' She has also written two plays and has two unpublished short novels. A translator of Portuguese, she studied literature at the University of Buenos Aires and has published Spanish versions of more than fifty literary works from Portugal and Brazil.

EDUARDO GUDIÑO-KIEFFER studied law at the National University of the Litoral, in Santa Fe, but gave up his practice to write. Born in Esperanza, Santa Fe, in 1935, he has worked for several Buenos Aires magazines and written seven novels, *Para comerte mejor* (1968), *Guía de pecadores* (1972), *Será por eso que la quiero tanto* (1974), *Medias negras, peluca rubia* (1979), *¿Somos?* (1981), *Magia blanca* (1985), and the forthcoming *Kérkyra, Kérkyra*, set in Corfu; and seven story collections, *Fabulario* (1969), *Carta abierta a Buenos Aires violento* (1970), *Jaque a pa y ma* (1979), *Ta te tías y otros juegos* (1980), *No son tan buenos tus aires* (1983), *Historia y cuentos del alfabeto* (with Hilda Torres Varela) (1986), and *Nombres de mujer* (1988). He has also written a children's story, *Un ángel en patitas* (1984); sketches of Buenos Aires, *Buenos Aires por arte de magia* (1986); and a political essay, *Manual para nativos pensantes* (1988). His story here is from the 1983 collection.

LILIANA HEER, born in Esperanza, Santa Fe, in 1941, is of

German Swiss descent. A practising psychoanalyst, she studied at the National University of the Litoral, in Rosario, and trained at the Graduate School of Psychotherapy in Buenos Aires, where she now lives. Her story here is from her first book, *Dejarse llevar* (1980), of which one critic wrote: 'A grey style and use of an almost bureaucratic jargon go hand in hand with a drab picture of the world, in which the cruelty of her characters only emphasizes the suffering of those who are ultimately inadequate and hopeless.' She is also the author of two novels, *Bloyd* (1984), which won the Boris Vian Prize, and *La tercera mitad* (1988), and co-author of the play *Ubi Sunt*. She is married, has three children, and is currently attached to a hospital where she works with terminally ill AIDS patients.

SILVINA OCAMPO was born in Buenos Aires in 1903, studied drawing and painting (at one point with Giorgio de Chirico, in Paris), and did not publish her first book until 1937. Her highly acclaimed poetry (Borges called her 'one of the greatest poets in the Spanish language') is collected in *Enumeración de la patria* (1942), which won a Municipal Prize; *Espacios métricos* (1945); *Sonetos del jardín* (1947); *Poemas de amor desesperado* (1949); *Los nombres* (1953), which was awarded the Second National Prize; *Lo amargo por dulce* (1962), which won the First National Prize; and *Amarillo celeste* (1972). Her stories, many only a few pages long, make few concessions to external reality or conventional values. They are published in the following: *Viaje olvidado* (1937), *Autobiografía de Irene* (1948), *La furia* (1959), *Las invitadas* (1961), *Los días de la noche* (1970), *Y así sucesivamente* (1987), from which her story here comes, and *Cornelia frente al espejo* (1988). A selection of early work, prefaced by Borges, has recently been published in English as *Leopoldina's Dream* (1988). She has also written a verse play with J. R. Wilcock, *Los traidores* (1956); a detective novel, *Los que aman, odian* (1962), with her husband Adolfo Bioy-Casares; a collection of children's stories, *La naranja maravillosa* (1977); and a book of poems on trees, *Ar-*

boles de Buenos Aires (1979), with photographs by Aldo Sessa. With her husband and Borges she edited the *Antología de la literatura fantástica* (1940) and the *Antología poética argentina* (1941). In 1976, she was awarded a Guggenheim Fellowship. She has also published a translation of Emily Dickinson. *Encuentros con Silvina Ocampo* (1982) is a book of conversations with the writer Noemí Ulla. Silvina Ocampo is a younger sister of Victoria, who in 1930 founded Argentina's landmark literary magazine *Sur*.

FERNANDO SÁNCHEZ-SORONDO was born in Buenos Aires in 1943 and until recently worked in advertising. He has also been a publicist for a publisher and currently, while teaching a writing workshop, he devotes himself exclusively to authorship. He has written two books of short stories, *Por orden de azar* (1965) and *El corte* (1981). The former won a Third National Prize; his story here is from the latter. He is also the author of the novels *Piedra libre para Flavia* (1968), *Jardín de invierno* (1976), *Risas y aplausos* (1980), and *Ampolla* (1984); and the poetry collections *Salpicón las más noches* (1974) and *Primeros auxilios* (1987).

FERNANDO SORRENTINO has been a school teacher, published a book of conversations with Borges, annotated several classics of Spanish and Argentine literature, compiled a number of anthologies of Argentine stories, and written seven volumes of short fiction, some of it for children and much of it in a humorous vein. These are: *La regresión zoológica* (1969), *Imperios y servidumbres* (1972), *El mejor de los mundos posibles* (1976), *Cuentos del mentiroso* (1978), *Sanitarios centenarios* (1979), *En defensa propia* (1982), and *El remedio para el rey ciego* (1984). The 1976 book won a Second Municipal Prize. A short novel and six tales were recently published in English under the title *Sanitary Centennial and Selected Short Stories*. Born in Buenos Aires in 1942, Sorrentino trained to teach Spanish,

Latin, and literature after a false start in law. His story here is from his 1984 collection, a reworking of old tales from various cultures. Sorrentino now runs a small printing business and together with the writer Juan José Delaney edits a story magazine called *Lucanor*.

SANTIAGO SYLVESTER was born in Salta, in the far north of Argentina, in 1942. At the age of seventeen he went to live in Buenos Aires for ten years, where he studied law and worked as a journalist. In 1969, he returned to Salta to practise law and also became cultural affairs director at the National University there. After the military take-over in 1976 he left Argentina for Madrid, where he has lived with his wife and two children since 1978. Essentially a poet, he has to date published seven volumes of verse: *En estos días* (1963); *El aire y su camino* (1966); *Esa fácil corona* (1971), *Palabra intencional* (1974); *La realidad provisoria* (1977); *Libro de viaje* (1982); and *Perro de laboratorio* (1987), about vivisection. Or is it a metaphor for the suffering of tortured human beings under the military dictatorship? His story collection *La prima carnal*, whose title story appears here, came out in 1986. His work has won awards in Salta, in Buenos Aires, and in Spain.

ALBERTO VANASCO wrote his first novel, *Justo en la cruz del camino* (1943), at the age of eighteen. His next, *Sin embargo Juan vivía* (1947), scarcely noticed when it appeared under the imprint of the HIGO Club (standing for 'Hostel of Intelligence, Grace [i.e., Wit], and Originality'), turned out to be a forerunner of the objectivist novel later taken up by a wave of French novelists. It was followed by *Para ellos la eternidad* (1957), *Los muchos que no viven* (1964), *Nueva York – Nueva York* (1967), *Otros verán el mar* (1977), and *Al sur del Río Grande* (1987), recent winner of one of Argentina's most important prizes. His principal verse is contained in *Ella en general* (1954) and *Canto rodado* (1962). In 1948, with the poet

Mario Trejo, Vanasco wrote the play *No hay piedad para Hamlet*, which won two major prizes. A pioneer of Latin-American science-fiction, his complete stories in this genre, *Memorias del futuro*, appeared in 1986. He has also written a book-length essay, *Vida y obra de Hegel* (1973). His story here is from *Los años infames* (1983), the so-called Infamous Decade that began when General Uriburu seized power in 1930. Vanasco was born in Buenos Aires in 1925 and later lived in the poor western province of San Juan, where his grand-father had a farm. In 1934, he moved back to Buenos Aires. Vanasco has worked for the Transport Authority, in the law courts, and on the docks; he has also taught mathematics, driven hire cars, been a journalist, and translated work by J.D. Salinger, James Agee, and Henry James. He has lived and worked in New York, Barcelona, and São Paulo.

SUSAN ASHE, the co-translator, was born in 1939 in northern India, where her father worked for the Indian government. After Independence, she came to live in England, and in 1958 went to St Andrews University to read French. She had previously studied French at Grenoble and German at Freiburg im Breisgau; later, she studied Italian and Spanish. Her translations have appeared in various periodicals and have been broadcast by the BBC. Her version of Grazia Deledda's novel *After the Divorce* was published in London in 1985. She has worked with Norman Thomas di Giovanni on translations of such Latin-American writers as Augusto Monterroso, Mario Vargas Llosa, and Jorge Luis Borges. She lives in Devon, where she has written a children's book and is at work on a third novel.

NORMAN THOMAS DI GIOVANNI, the editor, worked with Jorge Luis Borges in Cambridge, Massachusetts, and in Buenos Aires from the end of 1967 to 1972. An American, di Giovanni was born near Boston in 1933 and has lived in Britain

– currently in Devon – since he left the Argentine seventeen years ago. His translations of Borges have appeared in every major review and magazine in the United States and Britain. Much of this work was done in collaboration with Borges, and to date has appeared in book form in eleven volumes. Di Giovanni has written two novels – one, *1900*, based on a screenplay by Bernardo Bertolucci. He has also translated books by Adolfo Bioy-Casares, Syria Poletti, Silvina Ocampo, and Humberto Costantini. He is presently writing a book about his association with Borges as well as being engaged in translations of several Argentine and other Latin-American writers. Last year he edited the volume *In Memory of Borges*, which was published by Constable in association with the Anglo-Argentine Society.